D1512030

PRAISE FOR GARY COLLINS

Cabot Island

"Collins' focus on an ordinary event taking place under extraordinary circumstances sheds a tender, respectful light on how strength of character can be forged at the anguished intersection of isolation and bereavement."

DOWNHOME

"The story is intriguing . . ."

THE CHRONICLE HERALD

The Last Farewell

"The writing here is at its best when the danger and beauty of the sea is subtly described."

ATLANTIC BOOKS TODAY

"*The Last Farewell* tells a true story, but Collins' vivid description and well-realized characters make it read like a novel." — THE CHRONICLE HERALD

"Read *The Last Farewell* not only because it is a moving historical tale of needless tragedy but also because it's a book enriched with abundant details of Newfoundland life not so widespread anymore." — THE PILOT

"[*The Last Farewell*] is informative and intriguing, and not merely for experienced sailors or Newfoundlanders."

— THE NORTHERN MARINER

What Colour is the Ocean?

"Delightful rhyming story."
RESOURCE LINKS

"Scott Keating's illustrations are an asset to the book. The double page illustrations revealing the colour of the ocean are particularly successful in conveying the moods of the ocean and the land."
CM: CANADIAN REVIEW OF MATERIALS

"This tale, set by the sea in Newfoundland, is told in a simple repetitive refrain that will capture the imagination of young readers. . . . Illustrations by Scott Keating, award-winning artist and illustrator, capture the beauty of Newfoundland and the many seasons and moods of the ocean." — ATLANTIC BOOKS TODAY

Soulis Joe's Lost Mine

"There is a magic in the interior of this island that few will write about or speak of to others—an endless fascination with the land. Gary Collins is entranced in the same way that the allure of rock, tree, and bog seized the indomitable Allan Keats, and before him, his ancestor, the Mi'kmaq Soulis Joe. This book gives voice not only to these men but to the great and wonderful wilderness of Newfoundland. Read it and be prepared for the wonder and love of the wild places. It will grab and hold on to you, too."
J.A. RICKETTS, AUTHOR OF *THE BADGER RIOT*

"*Soulis Joe's Lost Mine* is a number of stories in one: it's a great mystery-adventure; it's a fascinating look at prospecting for precious metals; and it's a heart-warming story about the importance of family pride."
THE CHRONICLE HERALD

"This tale also serves to cement Collins' status as one of the region's better storytellers; he has a journalist's eye for detail, his writing is crisp and lean and the narrative arc runs smooth and seamless and is well-peppered with shakes of home-spun humour."
ATLANTIC BOOKS TODAY

Where Eagles Lie Fallen

"Some truly breathtaking stories of tragedy . . ."
THE NORTHEAST AVALON TIMES

"A gripping story,
which cuts to the true heart of tragedy."
DOWNHOME

Mattie Mitchell:
Newfoundland's Greatest Frontiersman

"[Gary Collins] weaves the various threads of the story into a marvellous yarn—all the more marvellous because it is true."
THE NORTHEAST AVALON TIMES

A Day on the Ridge

"The 22 pieces in [*A Day on the Ridge*] vary considerably: a serious accident to a man canoeing with a friend down a remote and dangerous river; the life and death of a big bull moose; coming home from the woods for Christmas; the New Year's Day Orange Parade and getting caught in an otter trap—and escaping from it. Every one of these pieces is exciting and well worth reading; each is well-written, too. This may be Collins' best book, though his other six rank high, too." — THE PEI GUARDIAN

The Gale of 1929

"This book is gripping . . ."
THE PEI GUARDIAN

"Not unlike the seasoned schoonermen battling the famous gale, Collins manages to navigate his way around each story as seen through the eyes of the characters involved. It may be that I, myself, had an affinity for the characters, having been through a similar situation on a 115-foot schooner. But, it felt to me like Collins took me up and down each wave, and let me inside each heroic task of survival."
ARTS EAST

Left to Die

"Gary Collins has written a powerful, gut-wrenching book that, at least, deserves a place on the same bookshelf as *Death on the Ice*, if not on a shelf above."
THE SOUTHERN GAZETTE

"Gary Collins delivers a powerful reminder that the 1914 sealing disaster shouldn't be dismissed as an act of God or a freak tragedy. The men on the SS Newfoundland, and their fathers and grandfathers before them, faced treacherous working conditions and risked their lives every year just to get by. *Left to Die* helps to ensure that their struggle and stories will be remembered." — CANADA'S HISTORY

A Time That Was

"Collins's gift is that of capturing real people and real lives." — THE NORTHEAST AVALON TIMES

"A book to re-read every Christmas."
THE PEI GUARDIAN

"Readers disheartened by the panic shopping and often forced conviviality of the holiday season will rejoice in the sagas of family, community, triumph and travail that native Newfoundland writer Gary Collins delivers in *A Time That Was*." — THE CHRONICLE HERALD

Desperation:
The Queen of Swansea

"I loved this book, I could find no fault with it, no low points, no extraneous material and, certainly, no boring passages or ramblings. Mr. Collins is clearly at the top of his storytelling game." — THE MIRAMICHI READER

"*Desperation: The Queen of Swansea* is a must read."
EDWARDS BOOK CLUB

THE LAST
BEOTHUK

BY GARY COLLINS

THE LAST BEOTHUK

GARY COLLINS

FLANKER PRESS LIMITED
ST. JOHN'S

Library and Archives Canada Cataloguing in Publication

Collins, Gary, 1949-, author
The Last Beothuk / Gary Collins.

Includes bibliographic references.
Issued in print and electronic formats.
ISBN 978-1-77117-632-3 (paperback).--ISBN 978-1-77117-633-0
(epub).--ISBN 978-1-77117-634-7 (kindle).--ISBN 978-1-77117-635-4 (pdf)

A CIP catalogue record for this book is available from Library and Archives Canada.

PRINTED IN CANADA

This paper has been certified to meet the environmental and social standards of the Forest Stewardship Council® (FSC®) and comes from responsibly managed forests, and verified recycled sources.

Cover Design by Graham Blair

FLANKER PRESS LTD.
PO BOX 2522, STATION C
ST. JOHN'S, NL
CANADA

TELEPHONE: (709) 739-4477   FAX: (709) 739-4420   TOLL-FREE: 1-866-739-4420
WWW.FLANKERPRESS.COM

9 8 7 6 5 4 3 2 1

We acknowledge the financial support of the Government of Canada through the Canada Book Fund (CBF) and the Government of Newfoundland and Labrador, Department of Tourism, Culture, Industry and Innovation for our publishing activities. We acknowledge the support of the Canada Council for the Arts, which last year invested $157 million to bring the arts to Canadians throughout the country. *Nous remercions le Conseil des arts du Canada de son soutien. L'an dernier, le Conseil a investi 157 millions de dollars pour mettre de l'art dans la vie des Canadiennes et des Canadiens de tout le pays.*

I dedicate this book to Janine—my niece, my friend—who has so skilfully "encapsulated" each one of my books and who has long sought her indigenous roots.

THE LAST
BEOTHUK

1

THERE WAS A sudden blur beneath the dripping boughs. The plump *kosweet's* left front leg had just reached the full extent of its reach, when a sleek, burnt, black-tipped spear punctured the delicate skin behind the shoulder blade of the unsuspecting animal.

For one heartbeat the deer halted, shocked into immobility. Then the spear sank farther into its soft fur. It went deep, between the ribs, and tore into a lung. The pain pushed the animal forward in flashes of grey along the narrow trail. There was a loud snap in the still air as the spear in the animal's side broke against a tree as it ran. The rest of the panicked herd sped away from the trail, the dozen or more deer flashing over the barrens and disappearing into the trees beyond.

The figure who stepped into the game trail made no attempt to follow his prey. His leg muscles were tense and cramped from crouching. Long before the dawn he had hidden beneath the sloping, wet boughs of the spruce tree.

It had been carefully chosen, hard by the twisting trail of the *kosweet* and downwind from the flaring pink nostrils of the deer, which had led the small herd. The hunter had let the young stag, proud and strong, pass where he lay hidden. The rut was barely over and the buck's meat would be tainted and foul-smelling with its sex glands. Instead he had chosen a female as his target and set out.

Cold autumn rain drizzled through the trees and settled onto the alder bush gorse and low shrubs. The raw wind that blew from the grey east carried the moisture deeper into the shrouded forest. Fog hung among the trees in gossamer webs.

The luxury of stretching relaxed the muscles of the tawny-skinned hunter. He turned into the wind and followed the winding trail the wounded deer had taken into the nearby forest. He wore deerskin clothing, which, with the soaking he'd gotten from his long wait, stank of old animal fat. The hide was plastered to his lean frame in dripping black, grey, and mottled white patches of heavy hair.

He had the easy gait of one born to walk, each effortless step the full length of his reach, a distance-eating stride, light and soundless. The slightly angular, hairless face was framed with a mane of hair the colour of a raven on a rainy night, the weight of it resting on his shoulders. The moisture beaded in his oily hair before dripping onto the warm, reddish-brown skin of his exposed neck. He was a Beothuk Indian, and he didn't know if he was one of the last of his breed on the Island of Newfoundland.

His brown eyes were deep and intense but hinted at wisdom and compassion. Now they searched the trail ahead, missing nothing. His eyes narrowed to slits against the cold rain. He left the low bushes of the barrens and strode on into the forest of tall spruce trees, following the narrow trail of the caribou. Spots of froth appeared on the higher bushes. It was a sure sign of a lung wound. He made no hurry, knowing he was on the deer's death trail.

Here the clinging bushes of the open barrens were left behind. The ground was covered with a yellow carpet of moss, with only the mar of the age-old caribou lead snaking among the tall trees, exposing the rocky soil beneath the floor. He found his spear shaft just past the first few trees. The break was red with blood. He caught the scent of the doe before he saw her, her smell strong and filled with death. A faint movement in a patch of ferns caught his eye. Moving closer, he approached cautiously, stepping around the back of the deer and not in front. He knew the smaller sharp antlers of the female were just as deadly as the larger of the stag. The cloven hooves were sharp.

The animal was lying on her right side, the wound from his broken spear barely visible, with only a trace of blood showing. The dying animal made a feeble, frightened attempt to rise at his approach, but the effort was too much and her efforts only caused a burst of frothy red bubbles to gush from her nostrils. Walking slowly around the back of the doe, the tall Beothuk watched the long pink tongue fall from the side of its open mouth. Suddenly, the long, graceful neck stretched out over the yellow counterpane, the short, muscled left leg stretching its length in unison with the death stretch of the head. The black cloven hoof kicked the air several times in rapid spasms before the muscles relaxed and drew the joint closer to the now still body. The black eyes of the animal remained open, staring, sightless.

Bending over the supine doe, the hunter picked up the head of his quarry by the antler and, satisfied the animal was dead, stood to his full height again. He pulled a stone knife from a sheath hanging by a leather thong around his narrow waist. Walking behind the fallen *kosweet*, he sighted along the direction of its staring eye, then stepped to a tree directly in

3

the animal's line of sight. He stripped off a piece of the bark with the knife. The black spruce wood exposed was damp and white. Stepping back to the animal, he grasped it by the antlers and pulled the head back until the soft throat was taut. Gripping the stone knife in his right hand, he cut through the warm skin with a brisk sawing motion. Instantly, dark, thick blood poured over his hands, and he quickly filled a cupped hand with the sticky liquid and walked back to the tree. Dipping his fingers into the blood, he made several straight marks up and down the smooth white surface of the spruce, facing the staring black eyes, making sure its dead spirit would keep following in the direction it wanted to go.

FROM FAR AWAY, the sound of rolling thunder came to his ears. The Beothuk trembled in fear. Not from the sound of thunder, but from the memory of another thunder-like sound which had changed his life forever. It had happened far from here, on the shores of the sea. It was a secret he had kept hidden, and one he knew he would soon have to reveal. After a while the thunder faded away. The Beothuk was still shaken by the memory the booming noise had awakened in him. He continued cleaning the caribou.

It took him close to an hour to dress out the animal to his liking. The paunch was pulled away from the carcass and discarded, the heart, liver, and kidneys removed from the viscera. He cut out the tongue and placed the delicacy with the animal's organs. His skilled hands cut through the neck vertebrae just behind the head, and making sure its still-open eyes looked in the direction of the marked blaze, he carefully placed the head on the ground. The deer fully eviscerated, he worked his knife between the animal's joints and skilfully disjointed the legs at the knees.

Satisfied with his work, he cleaned his knife on a bunch of wet leaves. Placing the organs and tongue in his skin shoulder pack, he bent down to pick up the carcass.

On bended knees he first hoisted the heavier hindquarters and then the forequarters across his shoulders. Grunting with the weight, he shrugged the limp load of meat to a comfortable position. With one hand holding the deer's legs tight to his chest, he turned back the way he had come.

2

He WENT BACK over the barrens, his stride slightly shortened with the weight. Occasionally he lifted his head from its bent position, making sure of his direction as he continued. Leaving the packed deer trail, he headed for a tongue of woods that snaked ahead. Entering the dense, black forest, he weaved his shoulders around the trees. The smooth hide of the deer brushed silently against the rough bark. On he went, following a faint trace through the quiet woods.

Abruptly he came upon a small stream that cut its way deep into the soil to expose the rocky bed it followed. The stream was narrow and shallow and bubbled pleasantly over its rocky way. He stopped in a clearing hard by the brook and shrugged the load from his back. He staggered a little from the sudden loss of weight. Leaning against a tree, he rested his back muscles for a minute. He was breathing heavily. He washed his hands and cupped them together to drink the clear water.

The area was well-known to him. It was a resting place that had been used by his people for generations. The ground was trodden and settled with use. Most of the lower branches of the trees had been cleared to allow better movement. A small firepit still smouldered back from the stream. Wisps of smoke were barely visible, resting at ground level.

Scarcely rested from his trek, he hurried toward the promising campfire. He hadn't eaten since early dawn the day before, and then it had only been a bellyful of overripe blueberries: tough, without juice, and nearly tasteless. He was hungry for the meat he carried. Bending over the fire and placing a few dry twigs among the ashes, he blew softly several times until he was rewarded with a faint red glow of heat. Soon a soft blaze erupted, and he added bigger pieces of wood to the fire and went back to his shoulder pack. Pulling out the large liver, he stepped to the stream and used his knife to cut off a piece of the viscous flesh. He dragged it through the shallow water several times to clean it and then removed the thin membrane of skin from the organ's meat. Returning to the fire, he placed several strips on the blackened rocks. The dripping flesh stuck to the hot surface immediately.

He waited patiently on his haunches while the meat cooked long enough for one of the pieces to slide from the cooking-rock. Piercing the meat with his knife, he sat back from the fire and gingerly bit off a piece. He swallowed the tender, half-raw meat almost without chewing, all the while keeping his eye on the rest of the simmering meat. After the heat released each piece from the small rocks, he pulled them from the fire. As quickly as he could, he ate all of the meat he had prepared.

It was still raining. The fog limited his sight through the trees. Water still dripped from his hair, and steam rose from his neck. The distant caw of a raven came, muffled and lonely. It was its flying sound. The hounds of the sky had found the deer. He was glad. Ravens always found food first and shared with the flock. Its calls always alerted other creatures to the kill site, though. The Beothuk wondered why the bird didn't keep its find secret.

His lean belly sated but not full, he prepared to leave the campsite again.

From the edge of the stream he flicked water with his hand until the small fire showed no sign of life. The rich organ meat had refreshed him with new energy. Bending down, he shouldered the pack. He stood once more with the load, his arms cradling the legs of the deer, holding the weight securely across his shoulders. Turning around, he studied the campsite, paying particular attention to the firepit. Assured all was well in this temporary resting place, he stepped across the bubbling stream. His step was more determined now, for there were other, smaller bellies depending on his precious load, which had resumed dripping slow, thick drops of blood upon his back.

On he trudged through the wet day until, far from the place of his last resting, he stopped, his labouring lungs demanding more oxygen, his leg muscles burning. Finding a waist-high blow-down, its dead branches just right to hold the deer carcass, he leaned back until the animal slipped from his shoulders. Sliding to the mossy floor, his back against a tree, he rested. He was breathing heavily and needed more meat.

Moving on, his way became easier. The trace he followed left the dense softwood forest and headed downhill through a stand of mature white birch. Here the going was good. The knee-high soft yellow ferns closed around the scant trail behind him, disguising his way.

The rain had stopped, but he hadn't noticed. When he heard the sound of waves washing against a rocky shore, he knew his journey had just about ended. The smell of burning birch came to his nostrils, and despite the aches in his body, a smile creased his face. Stepping around a clump of deep-green, shoulder-high alders that flourished between the massive birches, his eyes found his goal.

NESTLED AROUND THE base of a few high white birches and several yards back from the high bank of a large *woodum*—its white surface flecked with waves showing through the lower limbs of the trees—a neat, pale white birchbark *mamateek* stood, belonging to the scene, so natural did the manmade structure blend with the evening forest. Outside of the camp and to one side of the narrow opening of the dwelling burned a small fire, bright and without sparks. Loosening his load, he let it slide to the fern-covered ground and stared around the peaceful scene, waiting, a mist of steam rising from his sweating shoulders. Soon, from among the dense green branches of one of the spruce trees, interspersed among the dominant birches, a slim figure cautiously emerged, followed by a small girl who was only knee high to the mother.

The woman had a soft, slightly rounded face. Her skin was the same burnished colour as that of the hunter, very smooth and clear. Her hair was as dark as his and glistened from the recent rain. It framed her face before falling below her neckline. Her eyes were as brown as a cured beaver pelt, her smile showing straight, white teeth. She was very beautiful. The child who hid behind her was small, even for her five years, and was slight of frame, but her eyes were large, striking, and as dark as her father's. The dark eyes made the child look older than she was.

"The day has been long, Kopituk, my hunter, and your

step must be weary, for I heard you coming," said the woman as she approached.

"My step is not as light when I carry the full weight of the *kosweet*, woman," replied the tall man. "But it was the sound of its hide breaking a few small branches that your delicate ears heard," he added, his eyes lighting up at the presence of his family.

With a small cry of pleasure, the woman ran toward the deer carcass, which she hadn't noticed before. The girl stopped at her father's side and was pulled to his shoulders and squeezed to his chest with a hug that made the child squeal with delight.

"*Ewinon*, I have missed you," she said. And then in the same breath: "Where is the sweet frankum you promised?"

He placed her back on the ground.

"Patience, Small One. I have walked all the way to the barrens and back, carrying much weight while you have spent the day lazing by the fire," her father said in a voice that was gentle and joking.

"I have not been lazing at all!" came the quick reply. "I walked all the way to the brook at the end of the *woodum*, where the muskrats are, and I would have killed one with a rock but a branch got in the way, and the rat hid from me under the water—and he is still there!"

"Oh, you must be silent as *abideshook* the great cat, who walks on padded feet, and your arm must be strong and true to get the water rat while he swims. I will show you again, but come here now and see what I have for my Small One."

Bending before her father, the girl waited patiently with her small hands resting on her deerskin-clad thighs and peered into the dark folds of his pack. It smelled of animal blood, leather, woodsmoke, and green leaves. Pulling the caribou organs from the bag, her father dug deeper and brought out a thin pouch that was fashioned from the cured bladder of a she-fox, now bulging with lumpy contents.

"I knew you'd find some, I knew you would," the girl exclaimed, reaching for the small bag in her father's grasp.

Holding the treat out of her reach for a moment, he cautioned his daughter, "Wait, Small One, for the bag contains more than the sweet gum that I promised. See, here is the hard rough frankum that produces the sweet smell when held over the fire. Ah! Here is what you want, the soft, chewy, white frankum. Be sure and hold it in your mouth until it warms before you try to chew it or it will stick to your teeth." With this he gave the girl several pieces of the soft resin from the black spruce. Squealing with childish delight, she ran to the *mamateek* and disappeared inside the dark interior.

He walked toward his *woasut*, who was bent over and busy skinning the deer carcass. She rose from her work, bloody knife in hand, and threw her arms around him as his daughter had done.

"When you didn't come before the last dark time, I was afraid for you, Kopituk," she said into his chest. "And I heard the sound of thunder far away."

Kop's shoulders bunched, and it was a while before he spoke again. Tehonee, still with her arms around him, could feel his shoulders squirm and his chest shake. She knew something about the sound of thunder had startled him. Kop's shoulders always writhed when he was upset.

"What is it, Kopituk? Why did you tremble when I spoke about the thunder sounds?"

"I am not afraid of thunder, woman! My shoulders trembled with relief from carrying the weight of the deer home from the high hills." He didn't want to tell Tehonee what he had witnessed on the coast. He changed the subject.

"I feared for you, too, Tehonee, my *woasut*, and I was cold in the night without your warmth against my back. All the way to the high barrens I went before I found the *kosweet*. They have returned to the shelter of the big trees at last. This is good luck for us. We will have much *aschautch* to smoke and eat. And we will have new warm hides to wear in the season of cold and long nights that is coming."

Still holding the woman close against his side, he bent and brushed his lips tenderly against her hair. She smelled of woodsmoke and soft leather and a woman smell that was hers alone. Kop gently pushed her away, not wanting Tehonee to feel again how much even the thought of the thunder noise had upset him. He smiled at her. Seeing her husband relax again, Tehonee dismissed her fears and said:

"The tree-felling *mamchet* has found one of your traps again. Kuise was with me when I found it. It was only a young one. Its teeth were not yet yellow, and it had fat only in its broad tail. Kuise and I have eaten some of the meat, but there is plenty left for my hunter."

Walking by his side toward the dwelling, she suddenly laughed.

"Kuise roasted the heart from the *mamchet* on a stick and ate it all without stopping."

Kop smiled and said nothing, sharing the special moment as returning hunters through the ages had always done. Kop knew the telling of his daughter Kuise's eating a beaver heart would make much merriment at the next gathering of his clan.

NIGHT FOUND THE small family cloaked in its dark stillness. High above the quiet scene, tall trees brushed the sky clean, and brilliant stars appeared. The air cooled and the warm, damp earth smells rose and followed the small night breeze through the forest.

One of the scents from the camp was caught by the sensitive nose of a lone wolf, which had followed the scent of new meat all day. He was sleek and tawny and he was hungry. Turning toward the fresh smell, he loped along the old trail until he came to the small clearing. Here the smells mesmerized and stopped him. He caught the whiff of human and turned to go, but the smell of meat brought him back to the edge once more. He was very hungry. He advanced like a shadow, his bent legs lowering his sleek frame to the ground, his black nostrils sensing what he could not yet see. The smell of smoke rising from the fire halted him. It was the most hated of all the smells the Beothuk always carried with them. Still he waited, the closeness of the meat simmering a few feet over the small fire holding him. Then a long string of bloody fat fell from the meat into the hot coals. The hissing, guttering sound and the sudden flare-up startled the skittish animal into a blur of decision, and in one long, low, silent leap, he sprang back into the shadows from where he had come. Trail wise and ever wary, he did not come back.

Once during the night, the tall Beothuk appeared, naked, out of the lodge. He walked away, until his back was to the small fire, and stretched and urinated. Back at the campfire, he squatted and pulled a piece of the meat from the smoking rack and placed it in his mouth. Satisfied the meat was heated through, he placed a few more short birch sticks on the coals, and from a small pile already provided, he lowered a layer of green moss over the entire fire. It would now smoke through the night and help cure the venison into a tough, delicious food that would sustain his family until the time of the freezing moon.

He entered the dwelling again and the worn caribou-hide door fell in place over the opening behind him. The stillness that followed was broken only by several small whimpering sounds from the woman. It merged with distinct hissings of indrawn breath from within the shelter. After a while, all was still, save for the small waves that lapped and chuckled along the night shore.

3

THE LAST DAYS of autumn cooled and shortened. The ground became sogged with the frequent rains. And with only short forays around the sheltered campsite to augment their food supply, the need to hunt and gather farther afield was imperative. Some of the caribou meat remained, but most of the choice cuts had been eaten. The few shrivelled blueberries found close by were hardly worth the effort of getting soaked to the skin to find them. More abundant and easier to find were the firm red partridgeberries, but their flesh was still bitter and would need the first hint of frost to sweeten them. Later they would be picked by the man, woman, and the child by the baskets full. Mixed with venison and grease, they provided much energy. Some were allowed to freeze, and were eaten while still frozen. It was one of their fondest treats.

One evening, the wind faded away into the east and the huge pond was black with calm. Even the towering aspens were still, their yellowing leaves falling down through the branches, making a faint rustling sound. Every small stream gurgled and merged with the pond in a steady melody. High above, the clouds parted and the deep blue of the fall sky could be seen. From the east end of the pond the sound of geese were heard, coming ever closer. Hidden behind the trees, the Beothuk watched, his spirits soaring. The sound of the large birds was a promise of good hunting and food. He could almost taste the livers and hearts from the noisy geese. The honking grew louder, and now he could see the arrow-head shape of the flock as it veered down for a landing at the shallow end of the pond.

When they splashed down, they set up a loud honking that was a joy for the small family to hear. Looking around their new surroundings and seeing no threat, the tired birds soon settled down and began their endless search for food among the high grass, with only an occasional single honk from the ever-vigilant dominant male betraying their presence.

Kop couldn't see the geese from his vantage point near the campsite. He was separated from them by a long, low point of land that fingered out into the pond in a southerly direction. It was one of the reasons the campsite was chosen. Around the river mouths, game was always plentiful, and a camp too close would only scare it away. Pleased with the arrival of the geese and knowing they wouldn't be leaving their resting place this late in the day, he waited for the birds to lower their guard. The campfire had burned down to a few coals. Tehonee would not allow one trace of smoke to rise and scare the wary birds. The hunting of the big birds for meat was as important as the caribou. Waterfowl was a major source of food for the Beothuk Indians.

As the evening shortened, several other flocks of birds flew into the deep cove where the river spewed its contents. One of them was a group of whistling ducks, their small bodies flashing as they canted into their approach. Their noisy flying echoed across the still black pond and went rising up through the trees along the forested ridge.

Choosing shorter arrows from his quiver, Kop left the camp area in the gathering dusk. He left firm instructions for his family to remain away from the shoreline, where they might risk being seen by the migrating birds. Holding the bow in his left hand, and looping his leather quiver filled with bird arrows across his back, he left the small clearing and without a word disappeared into the forest.

He crept west for the first part of the way. Back from the shoreline, he followed an old game trail that traced the waterways. Nearing the head of the pond, the trumpet of the vigilant gander grew louder, the sound stirring the soul of the hunter. He slowed his pace to a stealthy trek among the trees, his eyes mindful of his footing, knowing the smallest sound would alarm the geese. He stepped on nothing he could step over. He was close enough now to peer through the smaller brush surrounding the pond to view the entire cove. The scene thrilled his hunting spirit. The end of the pond gave way to the mouth of the river, which twisted its way through the tall goose grass like a huge black eel before burying its head into the depths of the pond. Around the edge of the grass and swimming through the tall reeds were hundreds of ducks and geese. This secluded area of the pond was a favourite of the waterfowl, a place where they always returned annually.

The point was behind him now. His destination was in sight—the blind, long since carefully built, right at the water's edge where the river met the pond. He closed in on the blind in a crouching position and out of sight of the birds. This was the most crucial part of his stalk. Now several of the large geese were only a few feet from him. The hunting blind blended well with the dense growth along the bank. Still, he must approach with great stealth. The wary geese were not easily fooled.

Reaching the cover of the blind, he knelt on the ground

and didn't move for several moments, not even to allow himself to peek through the disguise at the unsuspecting birds so close at hand. Not until he was sure that any minute sound of his travel had melded into the evening shadows did he slowly part the brush and stare out across the cove. Here the current of the river had moulded with the pond. The only sign of its movement were a few red leaves drifting on the calm surface. Sensing the wind would come out of the west, the geese were swimming toward the dying light and coming ever closer to the hidden hunter, the vee of their wake barely showing in the calm water.

Raising his bow to the vertical to blend with the trees, he nocked one of the short arrows to the bowstring and waited. His line of sight was in perfect alignment with his aim—the whole place had been carefully prepared for this hunt many days before. The first bird that came into his view was the high-necked gander, its head stretched full and proud, swimming several feet ahead of the trusting flock. The silent Beothuk waited, his muscles tense, his eyes never leaving the male bird. The slack bowstring drew taut, etched against the right side of his chin. Never once did he move his concentration to the other birds. The gander led the unsuspecting troop farther along the shoreline, and just for a second it stretched its neck back along its sleek body to preen the coarse black feathers of its tail. And Kop saw his chance.

He pulled the bowstring all the way back, then loosed the dried birch arrow. The sound of its release was a mere rustle that went unnoticed by the other birds. The deadly bolt was fledged for only a second before it entered the hapless bird, where the neck met the broad chest, and buried itself to the shaft into the startled goose. The long, graceful neck reached toward the fading light, and the beak opened to scream its warning, but it suddenly fell and folded into the black water without making a sound.

Behind the dead leader, the first of the flock swam on and, showing no sign of alarm, approached the fallen gander. Several of them poked their long necks below the surface, searching for the food the gander had found. While many of their heads were underwater, the deadly arrows were released again. Two more of the big birds met the same fate as the first, and still the feeding geese—many of them with only their webbed feet sticking above the surface—raised their heads above water without any sign of alarm. Kop couldn't believe his good fortune. He waited for more of the birds to resume their feeding below water, then released two more arrows with the same deadly success.

In haste, now, he pulled another arrow from the quiver and, in the same motion, released it. Too late. He knew the shot wasn't clean, even before the arrow feathers flew past the neck of the terrified goose. The bird screamed in pain. The arrow had glanced through the skin of its neck before falling into the water with a splash. Racing away over the water, the bird clawed for flight, its wings battering the air for altitude. Now the cove was alive with the honking geese and the whistling wings of the ducks. The evening woods resonated with their cries of alarm. The Beothuk stood in his blind. There was no need for caution now, and he loosed one more arrow at the nearest bird. The shaft caught the goose mid-belly. Still struggling for flight, the bird fell sideways into the brush, where it squawked in misery.

Wading into the chest-high water, Kop retrieved his prey, which hadn't drifted far. He even found the arrow that had missed. Pulling the birds by the necks, he stumbled ashore, pulling his feet up from the muddy bottom as he went. He found the crippled goose that had foundered from the air in the tall grass. It cried out in fear as the hunter approached. Grabbing the bird by its long neck, he gave it a brief, humane twist, which broke its spine and stilled it in an instant. By full dark he was back at the campsite, his welcome greeted by cries of delight from his family.

"I heard the geese leave, Kopituk, and wondered if any of them had found your short arrows, though I never expected so many," Tehonee cried with high peals of laughter.

"I want *yijeek* of the hearts for my own," proclaimed little Kuise, laying claim to five of the tasty treats.

"You can have all of them if you can eat that many, my hungry Small One," said her father, already caught up in the celebration of a successful hunt.

Long after Kuise had eaten just two of the goose hearts and one dark liver and had been tucked under the warmth of her soft caribou-hide blankets inside the *mamateek*, the two adults plucked and cleaned the large birds. The outer feathers were plucked clean, and except for a few kept for arrow fletching and a few more for Kuise to use at her play, they were discarded. The film of down, however, which grew on the flesh of the birds, was a cherished possession to keep next to the skin of the sleeping child in the cold of the winter nights. The furry down was also carried with them and kept dry to aid in the starting of fire. Some of the birds had blue markings on their outer skin, stains from blueberries they had eaten.

The two adults feasted on goose liver and hearts skivvered on peeled alder stakes and laid across the small cooking fire, laughing as they burned their fingers on the simmering organs. The long necks of the birds were spitted over small poles which were fastened horizontally over the fire and turned to cook evenly to a dark brown. The plucked bodies of the birds were secured to the drying rack and would be dried and smoked, much the same as the deer meat, and then stored in birchbark containers. Such a bounty would feed the family for days.

THE COLD WARNING of winter came without snow or howling winds. The sun retreated into its westing much quicker and left its warm bed later every morning, making the nights longer. Then early one morning, when Kop reached for the hide flap of their lodge, it was stiff and cold to the touch. The cove was black and still, with no wind on its back. The pond was frozen over as far down its length as he could see. Squatting down to fill his arms with firewood, he shivered. Back inside where his daughter and woman still huddled beneath their robes of deer hide, he blew across the mute ashes until they glowed. With the addition of dry wood, the fire soon flared. For a moment the rising smoke circled his head as if seeking a way outside. It caused Kop to cough, waking Tehonee. The smoke straightened as it found the sooty smoke hole above. The fire burned bright and Kop chewed thoughtfully on a venison strip before speaking quietly to Tehonee.

"I wanted to return to the treeline this morning to hunt deer. But the frost has come and the leaves will be brittle and make much noise under my feet. I will wait for the first snow to make my way quiet."

"Your step is always light, my hunter," said Tehonee, only her pretty face showing above the furry hides.

"Even *abideshook*, the cat which prowls at night and the stealthiest of all hunters, will have his stalk betrayed by the frozen leaves under his broad paws, my *woasut*."

"You have provided well, Kopituk. We have meat to last till the snows come."

"A good hunter never stops hunting. The *mamchet* behind

the dam in the small stream which empties into the cove will be swimming in circles trying to keep his pool from freezing. If I can get close enough just before dark, when his guard is down, maybe my arrow will find one of them. Its fatty meat will add to our cache and its rich fur will make boots and hats for Small One."

"Kuise and I have watched the *mamchet*, too," said Tehonee. "He is a lazy one who spends all of his time eating and not storing the green willows and aspens outside his lodge, for the time of the long cold. Now he swims to keep the waters around him ice-free. He has waited too long. He will not win. Your arrow will save him from starving, Kopituk."

"It is our own bellies I am considering, and not the suffering of a lazy *mamchet*."

"Yes, my hunter."

"The frost will have driven the bitterness out of the red berries, loved as much by the cackling partridge as by us." It was Kop's way of telling Tehonee today would be a good day to gather the berries.

"The place where they grow best has already been found. Today, while you hunt the *mamchet*, who does not prepare for winter, Kuise and I will gather the red berries." Tehonee rose from the sleeping robe she shared with her husband. Turning to the sleeping child, she fondly tucked the fur blanket under Kuise's chin.

Standing beside Kop for a moment, Tehonee opened the door flap and looked outside. She asked him a question she had wanted to ask for days.

"Where are the others, Kopituk? They should have met us here in the winter *mamateeks* a full moon ago. I know you have been walking to the high knoll in the time before dark. Searching and waiting for them."

Kop shifted his shoulders before answering. She knew it was a gesture he made when he did not want to talk about something.

Kop had been asking himself the same question. Unknown to Tehonee—or so he believed—he had been walking up through the heavy forest to the knoll, which provided a view to the east, for days now. It was from the east several others of their clan, who were their friends, should have arrived long ago, as they always did after the time for gathering food by the great salt water had passed.

Kop and his family had spent the summer miles away from here on the windswept coast. It was the way of his people. They feasted upon seabirds and their eggs, silvery fishes that glanced in small streams, and others which flashed and rolled upon the beaches, succulent shellfish and boneless fish with many small arms, which tried to hide in the water behind cloudy black veils, to the delight of Kuise. More fish than they could eat or carry. It was the time of plenty for all.

When the leaves had begun falling, they had made their way inland toward the caribou herds, spawning salmon, and shelter in the forest from the storms which would come.

"Maybe their feet have been slowed by the weight of their hunting by the sea," said Kop.

"The summer hunt did not slow our feet, my hunter." Tehonee was looking out at the two empty *mamateeks*, which stood still and quiet across the frozen meadow, their skin doors closed, no heat or smoke rising from the smoke holes.

Kop did not comment. Like his woman, for days he had expected the others to arrive. The joyous shouts of welcome from the forest never came. The two shelters which should hold two other families remained silent.

"There were children with them, Kopituk. One of them a boy younger than Kuise, and your friend Buka's older daughter, Yaseek, who was so named because she was first-born. She is Kuise's friend. How long before you will go and look for them, my hunter?"

"When I have killed your lazy *mamchet* I will go as far as the tall pine pollard at the end of the valley, through which the rocky brook flows. From that dead tree on the high hill there I can see far. If they are on their way, I will find their trace."

"And if you don't?"

"If I don't find their spoor, then they are not coming."

"Do you think the rumours are true, Kopituk?"

"I don't know if they are true or not, woman!" Though Kop's voice sounded angry, he was speaking more from frustration than anger. He spoke again, softer this time. "Rumours are never true."

"You and I have heard the sounds of the Unwanted Ones, Kopituk. The thunder sounds without rain or clouds are not rumours. The elders have told us of strange boats on the sea. They have seen strange men, too. There are tales of our people carried away in these strange boats many times, and they have never returned. Each season when we return from the coast, more and more of our people are missing. But you will not heed the stories. Have you seen them? The Unwanted Ones, I mean. You ranged the coast for days, alone, after we heard the first distant thunderclaps from a clear blue sky. Did you see the Unwanted Ones?"

Kop squirmed again, and he turned from Tehonee to stare at the *mamateeks*.

"You know something, Kopituk! You have seen something! I know you did. You are not telling me all you saw by the salt water, where the small fishes offer themselves upon the beaches!" Tehonee swung around till she faced Kop full-on, challenging him to deny her accusation.

Kop turned his head away. Tehonee grabbed both his arms and looked directly up at him, saying nothing. It was a bold move for a woman to make to a hunter. Kop finally returned her stare. Her eyes were beseeching.

Finally, Kop relented. His breath burst from his lips, as if he were relieved to finally share the secret he had kept inside for months. "Yes, Tehonee. I did see something, something which I do not understand. It has worried me because I do not know exactly what it was I saw. I did not tell you because of that and because there was no need to worry you, too."

"We share in all things, Kopituk, man to woman. Woman to man. It is our way. Even the worries we share together. When the worry of one is shared by two, already it becomes weakened."

"You remember the day when we heard the thunder come out of a cloudless sky?"

Tehonee nodded.

"I walked toward the big noise as far as the cliff above the deep cove, where the others were camped on the level grass above the beach."

Kop shifted again, not wanting to continue.

"I remember the day well. We were frightened by the thunder sound without clouds. You were gone long and brought night on your shoulder when you returned," said Tehonee.

Kop nodded, and then he finally told Tehonee what he had seen last summer.

4

ALL THREE FAMILIES had journeyed down the same river valley to the sea. It was a wonderful time for them. The days on the coast were much looked forward to, as much for the pure enjoyment of visiting with many others of their clan, who came from different routes, as it was for the full bellies the great salt sea always provided.

They set up temporary *meoticks*—smaller lodges—near the mouths of rivers and above sandy beaches, where in late spring great schools of fish were washed upon the shore, free for the gathering. And among the frenzied spawning multitude of small fishes they scooped bigger fish, their bellies filled and their flesh sweet and fat. They threw addled eggs from the nests of seagulls to compel the birds to lay eggs again. All through that summer of plenty by the bounding sea, the Beothuk feasted and lived in freedom.

Then one day, Kop left when the sun was only a promise in the sky. He and his family had journeyed farther along the coast from the others to be closer to the place of the sacred red soil. Inland and along by a deep river valley, Kop walked alone for two full days. At night he slept under the shelter of overhanging boughs. Then he was directly below a steep red bluff long exposed to the elements. Here the red soil he wanted was presented in talus streaks, as well as in the drifts which had avalanched down the ridge years past. Kop spat on his hand and rubbed the soft soil between his hands, making sure it was the right consistency. His palms quickly turned red. He smiled with satisfaction. Kop gathered the soil in silence and placed in it a leather bag which he carried for that purpose only. He filled the bag to the mouth, tied it off, and left the valley and headed back to the coast.

He would share the sacred dye with the other families. The sun, red as a burning ember, emerged out of the great calm sea into a cloudless sky as he stepped along, filled with life and energy. To his right, the rote of the waves hissed and thundered upon the shore, retreating with a soft rumble of pebbles in a froth of white. And on his left was the mysterious green forest, where tall pine pollards, majestic and white, fluted above all the other tress.

THE SUN HAD lost its look of fire and was no more than two hands above the horizon on the second day when Kop heard the first explosion. Instinctively he looked toward the sky. There wasn't a cloud to be seen. No black, threatening storm clouds hurling lightning earthward. Kop was puzzled. The sound came once again. Then all was quiet. Quieter than it was before. The seabirds had stopped squawking, and the forest birds had ceased their singing. Kop was suddenly afraid without knowing why, and he shivered from head to toe. His step became heavy, and though he continued on his way, he crouched among the bushes as he went. Ahead of him was a long, wooded point, and beyond that a wide, deep cove edged by a curved beach many arrow shots long. It was here he hoped to meet the rest of his people. Without sky-lining his body, he reached the top of the point. The landwash, far below, was stripped of growth by the waves.

He was right. There, up from the beach, on the green sward was a *mamateek* and the smaller summer *meoticks* of his friends. Buka's *meotick* was one of them. He would know Buka's handiwork anywhere. There was no smoke rising from them, but two cook fires in front of the shelters were smouldering and in need of more wood. Why were the fires left unattended?

Kop was about to rise up and shout a greeting, when the quiet of the cove was sundered by another explosion. He froze in absolute fear. It was the same thunder-like sound he had heard twice before. Appearing from the point of land to his right, as if it had emerged from out of the cliffs themselves, over the ocean's surface came a huge floating apparition. Smoke was rising from a short black object protruding from its top side. Kop shivered in fear at the sight of it. What was it? His intelligence told him it was a kind of boat. It was many times longer and bigger than the biggest *tapooteek* Kop had ever seen. Growing out of the huge boat were two trees, perfectly straight and without natural branches. Tied to and hanging from both greyish-white trees was an array of lines the like of which was beyond Kop's understanding.

What Kopituk was seeing, and which was foreign to him, was a ship, a schooner-rigged sailing ship. The ship's cannon fired again. Smoke emitted from its hollow maw, and once again the sounds reverberated around the cove and up the cliffs, where the frightened Beothuk watched in awe. Men on the deck of the ship yelled and shouted as if the shot was one of victory. Kop heard a woman scream. He instinctively looked toward the large *mamateek*. One of the men by the shelter bent low and shouted angrily into the *mamateek*'s opening, gesturing with a long stick in his hand as he did so. The high-pitched sound of fear inside was silenced. Kop suddenly realized he could see not one of his friends. Whoever was inside were captives, but for how long had they been held prisoners inside their own lodge? And were they all, even the mighty Buka, also held captive by the Unwanted Ones?

The crash of the cannon died, and as if on cue, men emerged from the woods near the shelter as well as from the *mamateek* itself, two of whom stood by the *mamateek* opening as if they were on guard. The two men each held long, staff-like objects which looked like weapons that glinted when they moved. Kop was astonished by what he was seeing. A boat was drawn up over the beach just out of sight below the Beothuk camp. He had not noticed the boat before. As he watched from his place of hiding, the ship made ready to lower her sails. From her deck, men scrambled about and great shouts erupted from them—none of which the watching Beothuk understood. Men dressed in strange robes, from unruly heads to long boots, hauled on ropes and shouted as if possessed. And the sails attached to the poles came clattering down. More shouting was heard, and from one side of the ship's bow came a huge claw-like object. It fell into the water with a loud splash. It was followed by a clanking, rumbling sound out the hawse-hole, which further unnerved Kop. The chain stopped its run and straightened out in front of the ship. And as sudden as a floating tree on a swollen river was snagged by one of its own branches, so was the ship brought to heel by its iron hawser.

Four men went scurrying down the beach, climbed aboard a smaller boat, and promptly sat down on the thwarts. They all carried the iron staffs with them. Four long oars appeared in their hands, and the boat was pulled toward the waiting ship. The two men standing near the lodge flap had not moved.

Kop, numb with fear but determined to learn what was happening, crept closer to the beach. The boat returned, crowded with men. They jumped out of the boat and hauled it onto the beach directly below the *mamateeks*. The campfire outside the lodges was starving for fuel. Kop was close enough now to see large fish pierced on the spit above the simmering ashes and others on rocks placed beside the campfire. Smaller fishes had already been roasted to a golden brown. Kop could smell their savoury flesh. Men from the boat walked briskly up the beach and stopped in front of the two men who guarded the Beothuk camp. All except one of them carried the long black sticks in their hands. The one who did not was shorter than the others but powerfully built and had an authoritative air about him. He spoke in a growl to the two guards, who answered in the same harsh tongue. As if doubting their reply, their chief—Kop was sure he was their chief—turned his head to look all around the cove. His stare seemed to pierce the bushes where Kop was lying. Further shocked by that staring face, Kop buried his head in the ground and for a heartbeat he thought he was discovered. When he looked up again, the man's back was to him again, but Kop's stomach churned in turmoil at the face he had seen.

It was covered in the red spirit colour of his people.

TEHONEE GASPED WHEN she heard this, and Kop halted his narrative. But Tehonee would not be denied.

"Speak again, Kopituk. Buka and the others. What did you see of them and have not told me?"

Kop, visibly shaken by the telling of it, but seemingly now wanting to share the horrors he had kept hidden from Tehonee for a full season, continued.

He whose face was covered with hair and stained red

shouted at the two guards standing by, and the others gathered around him before strolling down the beach toward the boat. Now he was close enough to see clearly. His head and face and even his neck were covered with hair. Red hair. Where no hair grew, his face was covered in red blotches, as if he had done a poor job of staining his skin. Kop was astonished. One of the men who stood at the entrance to the *mamateek* began tying the deerskin flap closed, beginning at the top. Screams erupted from inside, and now Kop identified the voices of his friends. The red-haired man yelled what appeared to be an order at the men standing guard. The second of the guards, with hair the colour of bog mud, crouched into the opening and pointed the stick in his hand inside. It burst into a tongue of flame and smoke, accompanied by a muffled explosion. The screams stopped.

It was followed by a yell coming not from the *mamateek*, but from the forest edge beyond the camp clearing. It was a cry that Kop knew all too well. It was Buka's frightful hunting yell. Kop had heard it on countless hunting forays with his friend. The cry came again, fierce and confident, as if Buka had just made a great kill. The man who had fired into the *mamateek* seemed to be struggling with his black stick when Buka broke out from the trees with a blood-curdling shriek that was not his hunting cry. It was a cry of pure hatred. Buka stayed himself with obvious effort. He motioned behind him from the tree cover, and out stepped Yaseek, looking as defiant as her father.

Buka was naked from the waist up. His lean, sinewy arms were raised, and the rub of his ribs showed against taut skin. He had lost weight since Kop had last seen him, and his face was drawn. Yaseek, too, for all of her courageous stance in the face of great danger, looked haggard. The girl had lost much of her fullness. Kop wondered again for how long Buka and his tiny clan had been under siege. Somehow Buka and Yaseek had escaped the clutches of the Unwanted Ones.

Then, for the first time since their sudden appearance, Kop noticed Buka was not carrying his polished, iron-tipped spear. Kop had never seen Buka without it. Instead of his spear, in Buka's hand, raised high above his head, was the top of a budding pine tree. Its cones were a purplish red and swelling with seed. Buka was presenting the Unwanted Ones with a sign of peace! He shook the treetop and spoke aloud. "Returning from hunting, I have watched you hold my clan captive in their *mamateeks*. For many long days and longer nights I have watched and anguished over what you have done.

"You have carried no meat or water to them. Unlike the True People, you have shown much disrespect to your prisoners. Yaseek and I have not tasted food or supped water either, so we share the pangs of hunger and thirst with our people." Buka took a step forward. Yaseek followed. The Unwanted Ones, watching, clutched their muskets in a flurry, and the snicking of cocked hammers was heard. Buka stopped again, and Yaseek halted by his side.

The men shouted and laughed at Buka and gesticulated with their guns. None of it was understood by the Beothuk. To Kop it sounded like taunts. After the outburst had quieted down, Buka lowered the pine tree over his heart, to show sincerity, and spoke again. "Weak from hunger, the *munes* entered my head in the sleepless night." Kop gasped as he heard these words. Buka had communed with the spirits! Buka was a man of few words. Kop had never seen him talk so. The spirits had truly instructed him.

"Go with a budding pine, they told me, and offer it to the Unwanted Ones. But I am warrior and great hunter. I fought long against the *munes*, though it is not wise. To honour the spirits and to free my clan, I offer peace. I will talk to your chief, with hair the colour of fire; at the entrance to the *mamateeks*, where my people are your captives." Buka's voice was loud, stern and sure.

"By me, Yaseek!" he cried. "And show no fear!" Buka stepped forward, his head high.

"Yes, my *ewinon!*" came Yaseek's shrill voice, and trying to match her father's stride, she stepped forward and walked by his side.

There was a shout from the man with red hair, and a volley of explosions rocked the cove. Smoke from several flashpans burst into the air as the flintlocks opened fire on father and daughter. For a second it blocked Kop's view. And when it cleared, Kop saw Yaseek's lifeless body on the ground. Buka was bleeding, but his legs had carried him within reach of one of the guards at the *mamateek* door. His powerful fingers had closed around the man's neck. Buka kept screaming and choking the man in his grasp. The man dropped his musket and flayed his arms at his attacker in a clumsy panic. His blows fell on muscles of stone. He was going to die. The red-haired man screamed again, and the other guard pointed his own gun at Buka's naked back.

A spit of orange flame and smoke erupted from the gun, and a hole appeared in the centre of Buka's muscled back. His clutch of death was released, and his hands tried in vain to reach the terrible wound now spurting blood in runnels down his back. Without another sound, his knees buckled under him and he went face down upon the ground, framed in the closed door of his *mamateek*. Screams arose from inside the lòdge. The man still nursing his throat got to his feet and kicked Buka several times. The other man went inside the lodge. Sounds of a struggle were heard. The gun spoke from inside. The screams stopped, and the man stepped away from the lodge opening. The one who Buka had in the throat hold pierced Buka's body with the knife fastened to his stick-like weapon. And then they dragged his body and Yaseek's just inside the flap and finished tying it shut.

The leader nodded and crouched down, facing the *mamateek* with fire brands in his hand. Tendrils of smoke began to rise from the bottom of the birchbark sides. Flames rushed upwards, followed by dense black smoke and a roaring sound as the fire surged, feeding on the dry white bark. Pitiful screams of terror and panic went on and on from inside the *mamateek*. The Unwanted Ones ran down the beach toward the boat, where the red-haired man waited. One of them snatched some of the spitted fish as he passed the dead campfire.

The cries were drowned by the roar of flames. The structure soon folded down upon itself, as soft as a bough under the weight of winter snow. Kop tore his eyes from the fire. The boat had reached the ship, and the men were clambering up its sides. Shouts from the red-haired man came again, and the cannon was once more pointed shoreward. Kop knew another explosion would be heard. He steeled himself for it. What followed was something he was not prepared for. At the same time as the shot came, thunderous and very close, the cliff above Kop's head erupted with a small avalanche of talus and rocks, some of which rattled down and fell into the bushes next to his hiding place. Kop was stricken with fear, but he knew what had happened. The smoke and thunder from the ship had struck and shattered the very cliff above him. He knew this because it resembled the same smoke and fire which had torn the hole in Buka's back. On his hands and knees, he clawed away from the cove until, deep in the forest, he stood on his legs and ran from the sea as fast as he could go. He stopped when he became winded and sat in the concealment of a tall spruce. All around him were forest noises and nothing else. There was no one following him. Without further consideration, he made his way toward the coast again. Kop suddenly wondered if the keen eye of the red-haired man had seen him and the last thunderclap had been meant as a warning.

5

TEHONEE WAS WEEPING long before Kop had ended his tale. Her head was filled with questions. "Who are these savage people, Kopituk? Where did they come from? Why would they kill our friends? And to burn them in their *mamateeks!* And the one painted with the spirit mud! It must be an evil spirit, and not our gentle one."

Then: "Were they alive when they fired their home, Kopituk?" she asked softly, afraid of the answer.

"No," he lied. But Tehonee had seen his shoulders twitch before he answered her, and she knew.

"Be still, my *woasut*. I have few answers for you or for myself. We have heard of the Unwanted Ones for many seasons. They have been seen stealing salmon from our rivers in greater numbers than can be eaten. Killings, too, we have heard of, involving both sides. I did not believe all of it, thinking no one could be so evil. I know better now that my own eyes have witnessed things done by what must be evil spirits." Kop held his head high and looked away as he spoke, not wanting to see Tehonee's tears.

"He who wears the red soil upon his head and face does not wear it upon his skin." Kop spoke this last, as if he had just realized it. Tehonee wiped tears from her eyes as Kop continued. "We can no longer erect our summer *meoticks* upon our own shore, but will do so hidden among the trees, away from the beach, like thieves. We must be vigilant at all times and keep our guard when hunting and fishing. The Unwanted Ones do not fight as men, but will slay *be'nam* and children by fire. They are worse than animals. Even the wolf kills only for food."

He bowed his head in thought for a moment. Then, as if he had come to a great decision, he looked directly into Tehonee's eyes and said, "We must go back to the cove of death where they were slaughtered! Their bones must be painted with the sacred soil and then buried as True People. We must do the ceremony of the dead and say a *se'ko* over them."

Tehonee's breath caught in her throat. Her hand flew to her heaving breast at the prospect of visiting the place where so much evil had been, but she knew her husband was right. She walked away, nodding her head in acquiescence and much sorrow.

When Kop had finished telling Tehonee what he had seen, he left abruptly, telling her he was going down the valley in search of their friends. He had borne the terrible secret inside his heart for far too long. Kop was glad he had told Tehonee. He felt better, now that he had someone to share his grief.

Tehonee watched him go. He walked with his head down, and his legs did not stretch his full step, as was his way. She had known all season there was something Kop was keeping from her. Instinctively she had also known it was bad, but she had never thought it could be this bad. She felt as though their world was being taken away from them. And that for them there would be no refuge.

WITH SHARPENED SPEAR in his right hand and with bow and quiver filled with arrows across his back, Kop walked east down the trace. The long, green valley through which he walked and where a small brook ran was hemmed in by forested slopes. There were game trails on both sides of the stream, and Kop made good time. In places the shadows of trees laddered the scant trail. The day was growing short, and night was near when he reached his destination. He came out of the heavy timber and walked up the slope toward the dead pine tree. The brush was waist high and made a faint swishing sound as he passed through. Somewhere far away he heard a loon call as it flew toward a pond. Birds twittered and sang and a snipe hunted, its wings whooping in high-pitched skirls. The trunk of the great pine pollard, above its massive, twisted bole, was as broad as two men were wide, and stood alone. It was grey and stood like a sentinel on the hill overlooking the valley's end. Its shadow, long and black, dominated the knoll. The first of the thick grey branches, long since bereft of its green, scented needles, stretched horizontally far above Kop's head. Hand- and footholds carved and chopped in the soft wood were well used, and with their aid, Kop climbed the tree to the first of the branches, upon which he crouched and sat down.

The view was commanding. Long marshes, their grasses turning yellow, their deer trails darker and plainly seen in the evening, showed the wakes of swimming ducks. Moths, slowed by the cooling autumn, flitted around the pollard. A pair of woodpeckers hammered their beaks against the tree below Kop. They paused in their work long enough to listen at the hole they had chiselled out. As Kop watched, one of them jammed its beak inside the tree and withdrew a clammy white grub, which it swallowed before resuming its hunting. Its drumming on the hollow tree filled the evening air. Kop gazed long and carefully all around. He had seen no sign of humans during his long trek to the pollard. No one had walked the trail. He was sure of it. From this height he could see the glint of the sea many miles away. No rising smoke from an evening campfire. No soft sound of children talking as they came up the trail—nothing but the stir of birds and the drone of insects in the waning light. Kop waited and stared until his legs grew cramped and the light diffused his sight. Only then did he climb down the tree.

Casting all around, he searched for anything he might have missed. This place was well-known to the Beothuk as a lookout spot, and no one passed without stopping here. Kop could find no grasses bent, not one branch broken, nothing. With an aching heart, he bent his way homeward through the dark forest. Above him the snipe still hunted in the starry sky. When he drew up to his campsite, a glowing fire eased the dark. With an effort, he passed the empty lodges without looking at them. When he entered his own shelter, for a moment his tall figure was etched in the bright opening he had made. And in the still, cold night air, stark against the warm glow inside, his breath was visible.

6

THE MONTH OF new leaves had come with all of its promise of new life and warm days ahead. Snow still filled many of the deep valleys and clung to the north-facing slopes, but the back of winter was broken, and the scent of spring filled the air as the earth warmed for the coming season. New smells arose from the awakening soil. The treetops leaned and bowed to the warm south winds sighing down over the high, forested ridges.

Kop led his family up and over one of these ridges and enjoying the first of the long, sun-filled days. They had journeyed here from their winter house, having paddled down the long pond to its easternmost ends in their *tapooteek*. There, up a faint trail from the beach and nestled in a small clearing with a great view of the pond below, a *mamateek* stood waiting. It had been built years ago, and though it showed its age, only a few repairs were needed for the Indians' short stay. The pond waters were part of an age-old, much travelled route which would eventually lead them to the ocean.

They settled into their new lodge. After resting for a day, they made their way to a barren area, high on the ridge, pushed out of the dense softwood forest by some long-ago disturbance. It provided the travellers with wilted red partridgeberries, which had survived the winter. Their juices were now concentrated and, when gathered quickly, made a sweet meal. Tehonee and Kuise were busy gathering the berries and placing them in birchbark baskets. Kop heard the mother's happy giggles and the child's cries of delight as she popped the rumpled berries into her mouth. But he had led his family here for another reason. The barren rock gave him a masterful view of the pond, long and blue, as well as the sylvan valley below. He stood on a boulder on the edge of the clearing. It gave him a great vantage point to see the full length of the valley stretching away from the bog at the pond's east end. His black eyes were searching for something. They had crossed the bog below an hour ago, keeping to the high points to avoid most of the water. To the east and his right, the long valley reached far, the bog giving way to forest green. Heavy stands of trees sloped up over the ridges from both sides of the valley, hemming it in. Kop stared long, his eyes intense, hopeful.

To the west, the blue pond, down which they had travelled only two days ago, was now streaked with white as the warm spring wind raced over it. Trees were bending and urging the wind farther down through the valley. The same wind, which in winter moaned with cold, now hissed and soughed in pleasant gusts. A short canoe paddle out from the near shore of the pond was a small, rocky island with a sparse growth of low bushes and twisted tuckamore. Kop's gaze shifted up through the valley and always ended on the island. Searching.

The day waned and the sun moved farther up the pond, darkening the water and hushing the wind. Still Kop kept his vigil. His eyes missed nothing. A red fox, trotting across the valley in its criss-cross pattern with its head down, checked every bush and rock. Once Kop thought he saw the flash of a caribou on the edge of the bog on the north side of the valley. He looked away, then glanced back again. Seeing nothing more, he convinced himself he was mistaken about the caribou. His eyes were becoming tired from his long search.

"The day will soon be gone, my hunter, and the trail is long to our lodge," Tehonee called softly, sensing his concern. "We have filled our baskets with the red berries that have waited through the long winter for us. Their juices soak the bark and will soon turn sour."

"Fill your belly, woman, and glean what you can, and don't bother me with the sun's leaving. I can see its journey into the west. There is still time for our return, even after the light goes. Or are you afraid of the night?" His voice was harsh, his irritation plain.

Tehonee was silent. The tone of her husband's voice had hurt her. She knew he was uneasy. She went back to securing the baskets of shrunken and overripe berries for the long walk home.

Bending to sit on the boulder which he had stood on all day, Kop had hardly settled himself when he caught a sure movement just over the treeline to the east of the valley. And then they were there! The object of his searching eyes: several long skeins of them, the lowering sun glinting on their flashing wings, hundreds of seabirds clearing the trees and flying low through the valley. They were headed for the rocky island out in the lake, as he knew they would. The seabirds always came in the spring, not only to roost, but to nest on the island. It was what Kop had been looking for.

Winter was truly over. The birds flew up through the valley. They had come from a day's fishing on the distant sea. Soon they would lay hundreds of eggs on the island, each day making the trip back and forth the valley flyway. They would continue in this manner until their young had fledged. The first were the black cormorants, their long necks stretched tight. Behind them came a large wedge of shell-ducks, whose beating wings made a whistling sound as they flew. The sound stirred Kop's hunting blood. The birds promised good hunting. Now he relaxed. Turning, he stepped lively to where his family waited.

"Did you see them?" he asked. "There are many more sea-birds than last spring, and the lazy seagulls have not arrived yet."

"No, Kopituk, the seagulls will wait for the shags to lay their smoky blue *deliiues* first and then steal from them."

"They are much like us, then," returned her husband. His easy mood had returned with the appearance of the birds.

Five days Kop waited on the shore not far from the island now colonized by the noisy birds, waiting for the right time to approach the colony. The birds were flying around and over the island and swimming all around it. The trout around the island were soon exhausted by the birds, and each morning at the first grey of dawning, the black shags flew in small flocks down the valley, using it as a shortcut to the sea, which would take Kop and his family many days to reach. And each evening in the dying light they returned, their long necks swollen with saltwater fishes. Though their bellies were hungry, Kop wait-ed. He knew he had to wait until the birds had settled down to egg-laying. This done, they would not leave the colony, no matter the disturbance.

THE BEOTHUK CAMPSITE was on a gentle slope leading up from the lake. Virgin stands of spruce, fir, and birch grew there, green and dense. Towering above all other tress were the massive white pines, lording over the forest. High above the ground on one such pine tree, with footholds long since carved into its heavy bark, Kop made daily climbs. From this vantage point he could see the progress of the bird colony. For days he watched the shags erect their nests using small pieces of driftwood. Many of them were high up on the island, and he could see them against the sky. After a few days, the birds quieted down. The flurry of nest building was over. He knew the egg-laying had come, and the long time of devoted incubation had begun. He would wait two more days before visiting the colony.

Winding through the valley bottom above which the birds flew was a small, rocky stream. Throughout the brook's course, several beaver lodges, as well as many muskrat hubbles, were known by the Beothuk. Just upstream from the mouth of the brook was a beaver dam, built by the fat water rodents. It had raised the water level above the dam and had all but surrounded the beaver lodge. Below the structure, the water was slow and shallow. Kop slunk with great caution up the stream to the dam. He used the dam as a shield between him and the small pond where now, in late evening, the animals were swimming. It wasn't the beaver Kop was after this evening. He was after the smaller water rats, which used the beaver ponds extensively. The flooded area provided them with the tender water plants they loved so well. The muskrats had actually burrowed a nesting lodge into the beaver dam itself and used an underwater entrance. Kop knew this. He had been here before.

Peering above the dam with the setting sun to his back, he didn't have long to wait. Several water rats swam by. They were so close to his hiding place, Kop could have easily killed them with a heavy stick. But this would raise alarm, and he would get only one of the animals. Most of the muskrat looked like last year's young. Kop did not care much about their age. His family needed meat. His short arrows flew three times before the animals became aware. Flicking their scrawny tails in a puny imitation of the resounding slap issued from the beaver's broad tail, the survivors dived under and disappeared. Kop retrieved two of the dead water rats by reaching them with the end of his bow. The other one he dragged ashore using a long alder branch.

Back at the campsite, Tehonee was excited to see the animals, still dripping brook water. Kop handed them to her as if they were fat haunches of venison. The family loved the tender meat of the water rat. When they were done eating its flesh, only the white bones would remain. The muskrat fur was at its late-spring worst, so of little use for clothing.

Two DAYS LATER, Kop sat in the stern of their *tapooteek*, which had been fashioned with great care from the bark of a single large birch tree and fastened to alder ribs. Its seams had been smeared with hot pine pitch. It leaked some but was easily kept afloat. The cove was quiet. Only a few gentle waves lapped playfully upon the yellow beach. Tehonee, paddle in hand, was seated in the bow. Kuise squatted in the centre and could barely contain her excitement. She had long waited for this day when they would gather eggs. Aboard the canoe were a couple of birchbark baskets and one woven from cattail rushes.

Kop pushed away from the beach, and the canoe rocked side to side as he did so. Kuise squealed with delight. Tehonee gripped the sides of the boat in fear. She did not like boats. Kop saw her tension.

"Did you bring the water basket to test the *deliiues* of the black fish eaters, my woman?"

Tehonee, knowing Kop was looking at her, loosened her grip on the canoe. Balancing her paddle, she dug it deep into the water and pulled her weight, her fear of boats hidden. "Yes, Kopituk. And also large baskets to carry all the eggs we will gather."

"The winter has been a long one, and my belly misses the taste of eggs. It will take many before it is full."

"I will help carry the eggs to the canoe and eat many of them every day, my mother," said Kuise.

"Maybe the smell of the bird droppings will turn your small belly from eating even one egg, Small One," laughed her father.

"Maybe the thieving seagulls have left none for any of us," cried the always practical Tehonee, pointing her arm toward the island, where the raucous gulls could be seen and heard above it. As the canoe neared the landing, the noise grew deafening. The seagulls were diving down and screeching. The nesting female birds, with long necks stretched, were croaking and crying in fear and defiance, refusing to leave their nests. The male shags swooped behind and among the marauding seagulls, their voices adding to the cacophony now encompassing the rocky islet.

With both adults paddling hard, the canoe soon crossed the narrow stretch of water and hove to under the rookery. Below the island, the smell of guano was overpowering. Kuise and Tehonee both covered their noses. Kop stared at the screaming birds, which were now in full panic, and ignored the stench.

"I will shoot two seagulls before we leave the island and leave their bodies to rot. It will discourage the thieves from returning, at least for a few days. It will give us time to do our own stealing. When we reach the coast, we will take eggs from the thieving seagulls." Kop spoke loudly. No need for stealth now.

The treeless island loomed straight up out of the blue water for more than a hundred feet. Most of the cliffs were sheer, with narrow ledges well above the waterline. The sun glinted from a cloudless sky upon the water, and the cliff face was glazed with sunshine. Only one tiny cove, more an indentation than cove, allowed access from the water. It was here Kop steered the canoe, and the three stepped out upon the island. Though the exterior cliffs led straight up from the lake, leading away from the small cove, here was a steep, grassy slope up over the island. They lifted the canoe out of the water, and the three began climbing up.

Now the birds circled the island in a great squawking wreath. Their droppings squirted at intervals and came raining down, sometimes landing upon the heads of the three humans who dared disturb the colony. The smell was acrid. The crying of the birds and the batter of wings were mind-numbing. Only a few female birds remained in their nests, black necks craning, eyes askance, deep croaking sounds pouring from their open beaks as they reluctantly battered away from the nest and jumped over the edge of the cliffs. Below, the shags splashed down in the water and gathered in large rafts to swim around the island. Their necks looked even longer as they stretched to see what danger had come to them. Several adult ducks swam among them. And above it all, the raucous seagulls kept up their abuse, adding to the turmoil.

Now Kop and his family had to step lightly, for eggs were in every available crevice, and nests on every ledge and level space. Some of the shag nests were as high as Kuise's knees. The child's cries of delight added to the din.

"They aren't black, as they looked from the shore," she shouted to her parents in surprise. "They are blue and purple and have yellow feet, and they look at me sideways with their bog-coloured eyes without blinking. And their eggs are like a cloudy blue sky." Kuise picked an egg from one of the nests. No one mentioned the stink anymore, and the egg gathering began.

Chalky blue cormorant eggs—the most prevalent eggs— filled the baskets. They found duck eggs and even a few small, speckled twillick eggs. All were brought to Tehonee. It was she who would decide if the eggs were good to eat or if they were addled. She placed them in a cone-shaped basket filled with water and skilfully crafted from a single piece of birchbark. It was watertight. Now began a simple process well-known to the Beothuk. If the egg inside the shell had not yet begun its embryo growth, it would sink to the bottom, thus proving it to be edible. If it floated to the surface, it was addled and would be returned to the nest.

"We have come at the right time again, my hunter. Only a few of the eggs float to the surface, and even then do so very slowly," said Tehonee as she bent over her basket.

"No matter how slowly they sink, they must not be taken," Kop said. "They will stink and cause much stomach ache and vomiting when eaten. Only the ones that sink quickly will do. We have more than enough to choose from."

"Don't worry, my hunter. We will feast only on tasty eggs this night, without the fear of belly pains."

The gathering continued until they had enough. The rich protein would sustain them for many days. They left the island and paddled back to shore, and behind them, the frantic birds descended in great flocks upon the island. Above them the seagulls skirled once more.

THAT NIGHT THEY celebrated their good fortune. The eggs were boiled in a clay pot placed in the centre of a small, well-tended cooking fire. They ate with much relish and enjoyment. Kuise ate more than five. They cooked dozens of eggs and stored them away. When hard-boiled and kept in a cool, dry place under a mossy bank, the eggs would last for weeks and would provide much-needed energy.

Long after Kuise had fallen asleep inside the *mamateek*, Kop and Tehonee sat by the fire and stared at the starry sky. Their quiet talk was about the trip they would soon make to the sea. From close by on the lake came the high, rolling laughter of a male loon. The sound carried in the still night. It was a pleading, yearning sound. Before the echoing sound of the male had receded into the night hills, there came a response: the sweet, shrill notes of his mate somewhere out on the lake.

Tehonee wanted to know more about the Unwanted Ones, but it was a subject Kop rarely broached. Reaching down, Kop gently took her hand in his. Out of the lake the calls of the loons blended into one. And from the dying fire the couple rose and walked as one shadow toward their waiting bed.

7

THE DAYS OF spring lengthened into the first warm days of summer. And like the nomads they were, Kop and his family were on the move again. They had just reached the mouth of the river that ran out of the south side of the lake. Their small boat was loaded with all of their belongings. The spring runoff was over, but the water running down that river was still much too fast for a fragile boat with only a few inches of freeboard. Kop guided their small craft to the shore just before they reached the pull of the current. Tehonee stepped out into the water and pulled the *tapooteek* broadside to the boulder-lined shore. Kop stepped out knee deep into the deeper water and held it steady as Kuise got out and clambered up over the bank. Tehonee reached into the *tapooteek* for one of the hide bags.

"Leave everything aboard, my woman, and follow along the bank with Small One. Meet me at the bend by the still water beneath the dead pine tree. From there we will float easily down to the *woodum* of islands."

"Take care, Kopituk. The water is deep and strong, and the rocks are slippery."

"Many rabbits have come to the water, my father. Their

droppings are everywhere. And there goes one now! It is a baby one!" Kuise ran into the woods after the bounding little rabbit.

"There is no time for hunting baby rabbits, Small One. Just follow your mother and learn the trail as you go," Kop shouted in a voice that stopped Kuise from wandering farther.

Grasping the bow of the boat, Kop allowed the greedy current to swing it around until it was headed downstream. Keeping the boat in check, he followed it down. It was hard going and very slippery. He sank to his waist in places, and in others he had to manoeuvre the boat around rocks brimming with river spindrift. He stayed as close as he could to the shore, avoiding the strongest pull of the current. He allowed the *tapooteek* to gently brush by the rocks. A rip in its sides would mean a lengthy delay.

THE DAY WARMED, and the sun was high before he reached the steady water below the rapids. He had made better time than his family. The boat had pulled him along, forcing him to move quickly, and he splashed ashore under the gnarled arms of a great pine, seasoned grey in death. Here the water slowed and ran deep and still. The land levelled, and the river made its way in gentle curves through a yellow bog. The riverbank gave up its boulders to gravely brown sand and grass as tall as Kop's waist.

There came a sound behind him which he sensed more than heard, and Tehonee stepped out of the woods with Kuise trudging behind. Around their heads swarmed blackflies and mosquitoes. Kop had been swatting at them while he waited, without paying much attention to the yearly torment. Now he noticed the misery in his young daughter's face and the way she bore the scourge without complaint. It was a characteristic that didn't go unnoticed by her mother.

"We must have more red earth powder for Kuise's face, Kopituk. Too many bites from the stinging flies will give her sores."

"I hadn't noticed the bloodsuckers were so many. We will dab our faces with some of the red clay, though we must use it with care until we reach the saltwater coast, where I will get more of it."

"I know the place where the steep bank shows the small vein of red soil, Kopituk. It is many days' travel yet. It is near the place where you heard the thunder sounds last season."

Kop ignored Tehonee's last remark and said, "Kuise will not suffer too many bites."

From the leather pouch he always carried at his side, he shook a small amount of the dwindling red powder into his hand.

"Come here, Kuise," he said gently. The child came to her father's side, her short arms swinging at the hordes of flies which followed her every move. The brook murmured, the flies hummed, and the sun sparkled on the moving water.

Dipping his fingers into the brook, Kop stirred the red soil until it was a paste in the palm of his hand. Kneeling down, he beckoned Kuise closer. Tehonee and her daughter had walked hard along the shore strewn with boulders and overgrown with alders. The exertion had caused them to sweat. The voracious mosquitoes were drawn to their warm blood scent all the more. Especially to Kuise, whose small frame made easy prey. But she swatted at the flies without complaint.

Her father spread the red dye on her upturned face. He did it so reverently, it was if he were anointing her. Kuise lowered her black lashes as Kop smeared the red ochre around her eyes and over her nose and neck. He rubbed the clay on her exposed wrists, too, but more sparingly.

"This will not only protect you from the bloodsucking flies, Small One. It will also make you look even more beautiful." Her father spoke softly, finishing his work on the face he loved so much.

Kuise's face, her dark eyes staring and her white teeth shining behind her mask of red, was indeed beautiful. Tehonee beamed first at her daughter, then at her husband, loving his compliment.

They continued their journey downriver. All three of them now sat in the *tapooteek*, and the water gently carried them along. At intervals the two adults bent their cupped hands into the river and splashed water over their faces and arms. The cool liquid was a temporary relief against the flies, which followed them in a grey cloud.

Once, Kop lifted his head and sniffed at the air and grunted for silence. The *tapooteek* drifted with the tide as the three humans tensed as one, waiting. Kop spoke. "It is only a black bear that I caught the whiff of. He must be eating the new grasses. He stinks, as always."

"Maybe it isn't a he, Kopituk, but a she, and she has two or more cubs still sucking at her tender nipples," Tehonee said softly.

Kop growled a response that didn't require an answer from the woman. But she knew he hadn't thought about hunting the fresh young bear meat. Tehonee also knew it wasn't because of the danger involved in hunting for a bear cub with its mother. Kop feared nothing. But for some reason he was in a great hurry to reach the coast. And Tehonee feared it had something to do with their lost friends and the Unwanted Ones.

The *tapooteek* gathered speed as it neared the mouth of the river, and the current raced to be one with the pond of islands. Kop steered for the vee of the current, knowing it was the deepest, and they were carried out into the pond, where a welcome breeze gave them relief from the flies. They paddled along the shoreline, among the many small islands to the eastern end of the pond. Once, a sleek black otter rose up out of the water, near enough for a shot, but before Kop could nock his arrow, the animal had gone down. When it resurfaced, it was well out of range.

They paddled on. Kuise playfully dragged a stick through the water over the side of the *tapooteek* as they went. They passed several beaver lodges, but it was unlikely the animals would show themselves in the middle of a sunny day, and Kop pushed on.

Nearing a narrow section of the pond where the land was flat and low, they saw that abandoned, narrow beaver trails led through the water growth and to the forest banks, where only the gnawed stumps of hardwood trees remained. Tall cattails, their buds bursting, swayed and bent in the warm wind. Small birds flew and called. Insects buzzed above the water, and trout breached after them. The smell of a birthing summer permeated the air.

In one of the water runs, Kop spotted a family of muskrat. Their little water trails widened behind them as they swam toward the pond. Three ducks using the beaver runs for nesting sprang into the air and flew away, squawking a warning. The muskrat kept coming. Kop lowered his paddle, gave a quiet command, and Tehonee and Kuise bent over double and waited. The boat drifted as quiet as a floating log. Kop readied his bow, nocked an arrow, and drew back the caribou-hair string. The drawn bow made a slight twang when the arrow was released. The aim was true, and the force of the sharp, fire-hardened wooden bolt took the lead water rat just under water. The small creature rose up in pain and began swimming in confused circles, the arrow sticking out of its scrawny chest.

Another of the rodents swam toward it. It met the same fate. Its high squeaks of pain stopped suddenly as the black water filled its mouth.

By late evening they had reached the spot where the water flowed out of the pond again and continued through the land toward other ponds on its passage to the sea. They were now in a swiftly flowing narrow brook. Like the previous one, its banks were encased with boulders, and again Tehonee and Kuise made their way along the banks. Small streams of water entered the main flow and small streams left it, creating miniature tributaries twisting through the tangled underbrush.

This narrow rush of water caused Kop more concern than the previous river. Here the water ran waist deep. The bottom was uneven and treacherous. To allow more control, he tied a gad to the bow of the *tapooteek*. The twisted roots were strong and pliant and provided him with a short but strong painter. Twice he allowed his family aboard the boat when the river crossed long, deep pools of steady water.

Before the sun had done with its westing, they had reached their night camp. It was a place well chosen, where an elbow in the brook exiting a long steady provided a back eddy into a quiet cove of still water beneath a moss-covered clearing sheltered under tall spruce trees.

The travellers were weary and hungry. They pushed ashore and prepared for the night, which had already come down among the trees. The campsite had seen much use. There were firepits blackened with age and the remains of lodges in need of repair. Kop directed his family to one of them and began gutting the muskrat. Kuise walked past the dead firepits and thought how only one of them would glow on this night. Turning, she was about to voice her thoughts to Kop, but he was bent over his work, so she went in search of firewood. A fire was soon crackling and spitting. The skinned muskrat, skewered on sticks, was placed over it by Tehonee.

"Look to the roasting of the water rats, my woman. The speckled trout are feasting on the flies. See? The pool is alive with their breaching. They are fat and sweet-tasting."

Kop headed for the pool below their camp, carrying a long spear in his hand. At the shallow, lower end of the pool, where the dark waters swirled into eddies before merging once more with the movement of the river, three weirs and their rock fences guided channels of water away from the main flow into a small, shallow cove also surrounded by rocks. It had been constructed by his people long ago. Winter ice and the surge of spring runoff had done some damage. Standing in the water, Kop spent a while repairing the fallen fences. He was swarmed by mosquitoes. The water hummed and rippled down over the rocks.

Birds twittered and fussed in the trees overhanging the water, which were leaning in the evening breeze over his head. Kop broke armloads of branches from the birch and aspen trees. Their new leaves, soft, green, and sticky with sap, turned darker when he placed them in the water and worked them between the rock fences. Satisfied with the repairs, he sat on his haunches in the water. Flies buzzed and crawled over his face. From the shore across the river came the sound of his daughter playing. A faint wisp of smoke rose from Tehonee's campfire, and he could smell meat roasting. He was hungry. He stretched out his left arm, and as the voracious mosquitoes landed on it, he snatched them with the fingers of his right hand, quick as a hunting bat, and let them fall into the flow of the weir channel. The dead mosquitoes drifted with the slow current, and the hungry trout followed them into the trap.

Kop knew there were many trout in the shallow cove. He closed off the main channel to the weir with a heavy bough. The trout had no way out. He waded steadily into the water, which was little more than ankle deep. The trout swam away from him in fright. He crowded them into a narrow depression in the wall of the weir. Kneeling down with spear in hand, he began fishing. He waited until the panicked fish quieted into one slowly milling school. It took great skill to spear them. He had to be careful to gauge his thrusts just right: thrusting too hard could break the spear tip on the rocks of the weir. Many times he missed his target. But many times he did not. He hauled each trout, wriggling at the end of his spear, out of the water. He broke their necks and tossed them ashore. When he had speared enough, he pulled the bough from the weir channel again and skivvered his catch on a long branch. He walked across the river to the camp waiting for him. That night, the little band feasted. And on full bellies, they slept.

Three days later, with five ponds and one short traverse behind them, and with the sun high over their heads, Kop and his family reached the coast upon which the great salt sea washed. It was a time of feasting, warm days, and soft moonlit nights. But all Kop could think of was what lay ahead for him at the cove of death.

8

FOR KOPITUK, THE sea stretched into a huge distance of fear. Until the massive ships of the Unwanted Ones had appeared upon it, the ocean was a cornucopia of plenty. More fish and birds than all of his people could eat in the long, warm days of summer were there for the hunting and gathering. Kop's intelligence told him these ships had not been built here, on his island, but had come from a great distance down over the edge of the sea—and where that one came from, there were many more. Now his guard was kept to the sea—of which beyond its outer islands he knew little—more than to the forest, of which he knew all. His *meotick* was no longer standing on level ground just above the shingled beach where the sea murmured its ageless rote. It was now hidden among the trees and could not be seen from the sea, from which it was always thought no danger could come.

There were days when fog rolled in from the open ocean, creating swirling images of ghostly sailing ships, seeking the unwary shore, beneath the blanket. But Kop kept his vigil, and when the fog cleared, the ships were not there.

The days progressed and grew longer. By day the Beothuk feasted on the bounty gleaned from the sea. And on the warm summer nights they slept with full bellies under the brilliant stars tangled in the trees above. And still Kop did not lead his family toward the cove of death. Though he did not tell Tehonee, he was waiting for some sign from the spirit world to allay his fears. Anointing the bones of the dead with the red stain was a sacred process performed with much reverence, usually by an elder of the tribe. In the absence of an elder, if the dead one was a warrior and hunter, another of the same ilk could do the ceremony. Kop was known among his people as a great hunter.

"Buka was our best hunter, with the deadliest spear and the swiftest arrow," Kop said. They were gathered around a slow-burning campfire downwind from their *meotick*, in the deep woods just up from the curved brown beach. "Better he had died at the hands of the white bear which roams the spring ice than by the cowardly act of the Unwanted Ones," he went on. Tehonee and Kuise listened with bowed heads. Tehonee was about to mention Buka's hunt with the white bear but stopped herself in time. It was disrespectful for a woman to interrupt when a dead hunter was mentioned.

As if seeing into her thoughts, Kop said, "I remember well when Buka slew the largest white bear of them all with his great spear and three arrows, swift as one, sent into its beating heart. It was in the same cove where his bones now lie at the mercy of the raven and the sly weasel. Do you remember when Buka talked of that great hunt, Tehonee?"

"I will never forget it, my hunter. But now you must tell it again for Kuise to hear. And through your eyes she, too, will know about the greatest of all hunters."

THEY HAD COME down the river from the forested country in the season of budding trees and drifting sea ice, Kop told them.

Several families journeyed together to the coast, where they dispersed into smaller groups along the shore choked with sea ice. Buka and Kop and their families camped in the same cove. "You were even smaller then, Small One, and carried on your mother's back in a sling made from the soft hide of the fawn." Kuise cried in pleasant delight to hear her name spoken as part of such an important tale. Kop held out his hand for silence, and when Kuise was quiet, admonished by her mother not to interrupt again, Kop continued.

Thick ice drifted down from the north, and that spring, for as far as the eye could see from the highest cliffs, the sea was white. The winds blew hard in over the sea and pressed the ice sheets upon the land. In places where the ice met the rocks, the ice edges were beaten into grey slush, which surged back and forth with the tides. The seabirds were deprived of their shallow feeding ground offshore and sought out the black swatches of water between the ice pans near shore. They were so many, they cast shadows over the sun as they flew low in dense flocks over meadows of ice, canting and twisting in mid-air, searching for shallow water and food. The hungry birds found both near the shore, where the ice floes had grounded, creating oases of ice-cold water.

In late evening they settled down in the swatches by the thousands. So noisy was the ruckus from them, the racket sounded like the drone of a winter wind through a steep-walled canyon. And hidden among the rocky crevices downwind from them, Kop and Buka waited for the eider ducks to settle down. Buka shot his arrows first from a notch among the rocks without revealing himself. Amid the din from the birds, the arrows' flight was unheard. Kop nocked his arrow, and the two men fired bolt after bolt until their supply of arrows had been exhausted. Only the birds within range of the arrows were disturbed as they found their marks. They battered over the bodies of ducks alive and dead in a frantic attempt at escape. When the two men rose above the rocks, the crooning birds rose in panicked fright, eager to be away from the land, leaving behind dozens dead and dying. The two men dashed across the pans of ice like shadows in the twilight air. The black span of birds arched and dipped across the purple sky, seeking another swatch beyond the headland to the north.

Buka and Kop pulled the dead ducks from the water. They reached some of the crippled ones with their bows. Others had swum farther out in the swatch, and they were soon killed. Dark would be upon the two men before these birds drifted within reach. They would return in the morning and hopefully find them. They sped back over the pans of ice that dipped under their feet as they ran. Though heavily laden, they stepped quick as the lynx over the shifting ice beneath their feet, and never stopped until they stood once again upon the solid, unmoving land.

Buka and Kop returned to camp with their shoulders laden with the brown hens as well as many of the big king eider drakes. The birds were plucked, cleaned, and spitted on green alders. Fat from the plump birds fell and spat onto the coals. Their skins simmered and roasted and the feasting began.

The pack ice lingered for many days more. Once, Buka returned to camp with a seal he had speared by a breathing hole in the ice floe, where he had patiently waited for hours. He told Kop there were many other seals which used the same hole.

The next morning, before the sun had risen above the great white plain of sea ice, the two men were wending their way toward the breathing hole not far from shore. From their place of hiding behind a jagged ice hummock, where Buka had waited for so long the day before, it was clear there were many seals using the same air space. It was now more than a breathing hole and more like a small pool of water to which many seals came to crawl out onto the ice. Three seals had already pulled themselves out of the water, and on occasion others were rising up to view their surroundings. The two Beothuk lay still and quiet behind an ice hummock well chosen by Buka. The ice beneath them undulated and rolled with the swell of the ocean beneath.

The seals soon relaxed their guard. Pointing their black noses toward the warmth of the rising sun, they lay down on their sides and dozed. Without speaking, but with the signs known to all hunters, Buka and Kop made ready their spears and were preparing themselves for the sprint which would put them between the seals and the swatch of water toward which the animals would surely flee at the first sign of danger. It was at that moment Buka motioned Kop back into hiding with a downward sweep of his hand while holding his favourite spear with the long, sharp, metal tip. He had spotted something big coming over the ice.

The spear was Buka's prized possession and never left his side, not even when he went to his sleeping robe at night. He had broken the spear shaft twice, but the tip had remained intact, and each time he had secured it to another wooden shaft. Kop knew well the story of how Buka had found the wondrous spear tip. For Buka, true hunter that he was, had related the story many times.

Two spring hunts ago, Buka had hunted for seals by the shoreline at the end of a bay with a wide mouth. It was a favourite place for hunting seals. The ice was bearing down, and the tides swinging around the cape always brought loose ice, and with it, seals. The day was bright, and among the pans of ice, the wind was calm. Lying flat and hidden in his birchbark *adothe*—much smaller than a *tapooteek*—Buka was drifting with the ebb tide toward a small herd of seals. Some of them were dozing on the ice pans and others were bobbing up and down in the water. Buka's canoe resembled a floating log, and after a few cursory stares at the object floating toward them, the seals largely ignored the threat. With his head just above the side of the canoe, Buka waited for his chance. He sensed more than saw the time to attack, and barely showing himself above the gunnels, he looked out. The closest seal to him was a big male.

Buka threw his spear with all his might. The alert seal caught the movement and quickly rolled under the water. The well-thrown spear pierced the folds of fat on the seal's neck but not the tough hide. The startled animal dived completely under, the spear tip broke, and the shaft floated innocently above the swirl of water created by the seal's escape. Buka stood, grabbed his bow, and let loose two arrows. But the seals had been alerted by the commotion and were rapidly diving, and his arrows found water. Disappointed, Buka paddled for his arrows and spear shaft. He collected them and made his way back to shore.

The tide had brought more ice around the bill of the cape while he hunted, and he had to return by a different, much longer route. He pulled his canoe upon a gravelly beach, and with the light fading and growing cold, he decided to camp for the night. He was gathering driftwood for a fire when he saw an odd-shaped piece of wood, not natural to him, partially embedded in the beach sand, well up from the tide line. It was too big to start a fire with but would make an excellent backing for one. Kop ate his fare of smoked fish, relishing each bite. The sun long down, he crawled under his sleeping robe and was soon asleep. Twice during the night, cold seeped under his blanket and woke him. He added more wood to the smouldering fire and slept on.

The new day found him still near the fire and staring at something very strange. The odd-looking piece of wood had been consumed down to where it was buried in the soil. But standing straight up, with its end still embedded in the wood underneath the sand, was a long, black, and very straight spike. It was not made of wood, nor was it of stone or bone. The fire had not consumed it. It was still hot. Buka poked at it with a stick. Finding its base loose, he pushed it back and forth until it fell over onto the hot coals. It abruptly turned a bright red, but still it did not burn. Amazed, Buka flicked the object from the fire upon the sand. It lost its redness as it cooled, but for the longest time it still radiated heat enough to prevent handling. When Buka finally held the piece of metal in his hand, he instantly knew its value. It was longer than his hand and was tapered to a point sharper than the finest piece of chert.

He looked long out to sea, wondering where it had come from and what manner of people had fashioned it. With his usual practicality, he knew it would make the best of weapons. Buka spent all that day designing a way to secure the metal spike to his sleekest spear shaft. The first time he threw it at a tree, the bindings came loose and he had to modify them. Before the day was over, he had correctly fashioned the spike to the spear. Again and again he threw it at targets on the beach. When he tried it at the trunk of a tree again, it flew true and was so embedded in the wood he had to wrench it loose. Buka was amazed at his discovery and couldn't wait to try it. Next morning, he got his chance. Using the canoe again, he drifted out the bay among a few seals. When he saw his chance, he threw the spear at the back of a seal's head. The tip entered the seal's neck all the way to the bone. He used a braided thong of hair and leather fastened to the shank of the spear to tow the dead seal back to shore. With Buka's fire-hardened spear tipped with metal, his kills had increased and his fame as a hunter had grown.

Kop's musings about the wonderful spear tip were interrupted by Buka, who had caught a motion in his peripheral vision. It was not a seal. Something white and big was stalking the same water hole as they were. Buka pointed seaward. At first Kop saw nothing, only the shimmer of the ice blink to his left and the glare of the rising sun to his right. Then he saw it. Something white and massive was slinking over the ice between the hummocks. It was the undulating back of a huge ice bear. The bear was downwind from both the two Beothuk and the seals. As the men watched, the bear's black nose appeared above an ice ridge, seeking and zeroing in on the scent of its quarry. Both men dropped to the ice, fearing their excited breath rising above the hummock would be seen by the greatest of all hunters. The seals moved in apparent luxury, the blubber rolls on their sides pulsating as they languished between sleep and slumber, unaware of the danger flanking them.

A cloud smeared across the sky. Its long, grey shadow scudded over the ice floe and fell upon the seals. They raised their heads as one, casting around them, their huge black eyes rolling warily. Then the shadow fled down the ice. The bright sun returned, lulling the seals back to basking in its warmth. The huge white bear knew its best chance had come, and in a flashing blur of white, its four padded feet propelled it over the ice.

The consummate hunter, the bear's focus was not on all of the seals but on just one, the nearest to him. It was also the fattest one in the group. Less than a dozen strides, with its black nose flaring and its head lowered to the ice, was all it needed to reach its prey. The seal caught the scent of danger and screeched in alarm. It was enough to warn the other seals, but it was the last sound it would ever make.

The bear attacked in a full, relentless, deadly fury. Its left front paw rendered the seal immobile with just one powerful blow just below the head. It followed the vicious strike with a cough-like snarl muffled by a mouthful of seal fur. Just for an instant its jaws opened to reveal a thick, black tongue slavering between long, white canines. The vise-like jaws closed over the struggling seal's neck. Dark red blood from the doomed animal poured out of the bear's mouth. The other seals clawed frantically over the ice for escape. Mewling and bleating like fox kits, they reached the water hole, into which they plunged head first with a loud, clumsy splash and disappeared.

From behind their ice blind, Kop and Buka stared in fascination. They had just witnessed how the greatest hunter of all killed its prey. Kop was shivering as much in fear as with excitement. They were close enough to hear the suck of air escape the seal as the bear's bloodstained teeth vented its chest. Buka was shaking, too, but not in fear. The hunting lust was coursing through his very soul. He meant to kill the bear and signalled Kop his intent. Kop tried to dissuade him but knew it was no use.

The bear dropped the dead seal at its feet. Standing up on its two hind feet, it looked all around, claiming the kill as his alone. The ice was bloodstained, as were the bear's neck and chest. Its upper and lower jaws were covered in blood. The bear sat down on its hind legs and licked slowly at the blood on its paws, relishing the taste of it. It stood once more, this time on all four legs, and gave a furtive look around. It was hungry and eager to eat.

When the bear turned its back, Buka half stood above the ice hummock. Aiming for the sweet death spot just behind the bear's right front shoulder, with his long arrow nocked and drawn with its feathered fletch to the edge of his chin, he let loose the first one. Kop held two more arrows in readiness. Buka snatched another arrow from him and, with one fluent motion, nocked and drew back the bow and fluted the second arrow into the same wound made by the first.

The bear turned in surprise. There was no blood on its white fur. While it pawed at the arrows buried deep in its side, another sank in, just as deep, between the other two. The bear surged to its feet, and blood began pouring out of the wound. It clawed at the arrows and broke all three shafts. Now the wound was spurting blood all over the bear's white hide. A roar of pain and fury, along with seal fat and blood, escaped its open maw. Then the great bear's cry was muffled into a frothy cough by a surge of bloody bubbles erupting from its throat. It was then Bukashaman leaped from the ice blind with his long, black-tipped spear held high. His face was frozen into a fearless smile. His strong white teeth flashed defiantly. The frothy blood bubbles meant the arrows had ruptured the great bear's lungs. It was a sure death shot. Already the animal was weakening and faltering. Buka released a cry of victory that was fierce and beautiful to hear. And with his spear readied, and yelling all the more, he sped in a zigzag run over the ice pans. His long, black hair streamed back over his shoulders as he ran toward the roaring beast, which now gasped for breath and had red strings of blood pouring from its jaws.

Kop sprang into motion. A cry of triumph erupted from his throat. He was caught up in the hunting fever and the thrill of the successful hunt. The bear's great roars and Buka's yells split the icy air. Shivers raced down Kop's spine. He couldn't believe what he was seeing. Never had he seen such a sight! It was as if the endless blue sky and the great white plain had ceased all of their daily functions to witness this greatest of hunts.

A seal appeared in the swatch of water. It raised itself high above the surface. Then, startled by the screams of man and bear, it sank below the surface without a sound. The great bear staggered and went down on all four feet. Its once magnificent white coat was spattered, more with its own blood than that of the seal it had killed.

Buka, still yelling hysterically, neared the wounded animal. He crouched, his spear held horizontally, waist high, pointed at the terror-stricken bear. The beast raised itself to its full terrifying height as Buka approached. It had difficulty keeping on its hind feet. This was the most dangerous part of the hunt. The bear would die fighting. Buka stopped yelling his terrible war cry. He needed all his energy and breath for the risk he was taking. He knew it would all be over in an instant. Either he or the bear would die. He crept closer. The bear fell forward on its four feet, coughed up more blood, and snarled at the Beothuk. Its head was lowered, its ears pinned back. Its black nose sucked in air and blew out blood. Even its small black eyes looked rheumy and sick. Quickly losing strength, it forced its great weight upright again. The wound in its chest opened, and more blood poured out over its stained hide as it did. The bear shut its eyes in pure misery.

And Buka attacked.

He drove the spear beneath the flaring front paws, into the bleeding orifice. The bear roared in pain and swiped at its attacker. Though weakened by blood loss, if the bear's blow had connected, the fight would have been over for Buka. The swipe was close enough for the bear to drag strands of hair from Buka's head, but he was unharmed. He still held the butt of the spear in his hand. Another terrible, blood-curdling cry burst from his throat. At that moment he was a hunting animal as committed to the kill as was his adversary. And he knew no fear. Drunk with the adrenaline pumping through his body, he twisted the spear and thrust it deeper into the great bear's chest. The bear lunged at Buka again with both front paws, but it was weaker now. Its eyes were glazed. It was losing the strength to live.

Buka, buoyed by the thrill of the kill, jumped away from the animal. He danced and yelled and jumped around, just out of reach of the bear. Kop reached him, and both men cheered wildly as the bear fell on its haunches. Its breath was choked with blood. The great head fell on its proud, bloodied chest. Its massive body slumped over against an ice ledge, keeping it partly upright. The two black eyes opened. Both of its hind legs slowly stretched to their full length, and then slowly contracted back. One last breath gushed out of its mouth, and though the jaws gasped once for life, no breath went in. The great white hunter, with its once-pristine coat blood-spattered and torn, its eyes staring without seeing, was dead.

9

FOR THREE MOONLIT nights and four warm, sunny days, Kop had watched for a sign to lead his family to the place where their friends had been killed a full season ago. He had witnessed and even helped with the sacred painting of the bones of the dead before, but he had never taken control of such a ceremony. He was afraid to be in charge.

Then, one late afternoon when the sea was calm, he spied a fish hawk hovering in the same spot, for the longest time, high above the water without diving. Curious, Kop walked toward the best of fish hunters. He was sure the hawk was looking at him and not down into the water. As he approached, the hawk moved away, still hovering, and Kop followed. Flying just offshore, the stoop of the hawk drew him on until he was standing on the point above the cove where Buka and the others had died. Hiding, he stared at the silent cove and the beach, where only blackened debris remained of the once proud Beothuk camp. He looked for the fish hawk. For a moment he thought it had gone. And then it appeared, directly adjacent the burnt remnants of the *mamateeks*, hovering without diving as it had done before.

As he watched, the proud osprey fell seaward, its loud

screech piercing the silence of the cove as it fell, arrow straight, into the black water. Kop had never heard the fish hawk call as it dived before. The bird arose out of the sea, water shimmering from its battering wings, and hovered over the sight as before. Twice more the bird dived and arose out of the sea, just as magnificently, to the skies, where it continued to hover, its great hooked talons empty. Kop rose from his place of concealment and headed toward the beach. When he reached it, the fish hawk was nowhere to be seen. Kop had been given his sign.

THE SUN WAS less than one hand above the sea where it would hide for the night. With the light of the rising moon, which had a similar shape to the beach, like a strung bow, Kop made his way back to his family. He told Tehonee he would return to the cove the next day to carry out the ceremony of the red clay. She and Kuise were to go with him. Tehonee snuggled close to her sleeping daughter. She would not share the robes of the hunter, who with the new day would enter into the spirit world.

The next day, in the place they would forever call the cove of death, Kop prepared a sacred ceremony. He would not remove any bodies for burial rites or do any staining of bones before the remains were consecrated with their ancient ritual of smudging. He heated small red beach stones in a low fire before placing them into the hollow depression of a boulder up from the beach. Verdant, spiked leaves with earth-coloured undersides, soft as eider down, were tied together and placed on the rocks. With small reams of crushed birchbark under them, they were set alight. The green herbs smouldered without catching fire and produced a thick, blue smoke giving off a dense, pungent odour. Kop knelt and drew the smoke toward him with his open palms, as if washing his face with it. His eyes watered with the tang of the smoke. With his open palms he gently pushed the smoke in the direction of the rising sun and to where it would set.

Tehonee and Kuise stood with heads bowed until Kop beckoned them to him. Without speaking, they knelt beside him, and Kop wafted smoke over and around them. Kuise coughed once and her eyes watered. She was quickly silenced by her mother. The green leaves blackened and smouldered. The smoke died away. Water poured out of Kop's eyes, and he stood up. So strong was the smoke in his eyes, he staggered once. Tehonee gasped, knowing Kop had been recognized by the ancient spirits. They walked away from the place of smudging, not toward the blackened remains of the *mamateek*, where the dead lay, but into the forest.

There in a small clearing, in a natural depression already chosen by Kop, where the rich soil was soft and surrounded by high trees soughing in the warm summer breeze, under Kop's soft-spoken instructions they prepared a burial site for the bones of their friends. They walked in great reverence, having not yet entered the place of death. The leather thong which held Buka's talisman of ice bear claws and teeth around his neck had been partially burnt. The fire, which had consumed the family of Beothuk, fed by the dry birchbark walls, died quickly after the bark had been burnt and the black poles had collapsed inward. All of the human remains lay slightly burnt but otherwise intact. Buka's was the tallest of them all. Kop sighed with relief, knowing it was possible that the thunder sticks and blows from the Unwanted Ones had killed them, and not the dreaded fire.

They were dressed in their finest buckskins and moccasins, and their faces shone bright with new red ochre. The trappings of the dead—clothing, personal belongings, tools and weapons, including their bones—were stained generously with the red stain of the sacred red earth. Kop himself stained Buka's prized ice bear talisman before placing it over Buka's neck bones. Then he remembered Buka's missing spear.

He left the burial ground with a brief explanation to his family. He returned to the same place he had hidden on the day of the massacre. There he focused his view and his memory on the place where Buka had exited the woods without his spear. He found it easily and entered the woods at the exact spot. Now he walked carefully, surveying the area with a discerning eye. Buka would not have carelessly thrown his spear among the bushes. He would have put it somewhere he could easily retrieve it. Nor would it be far into the woods, for Buka would have kept it in his hand as long as possible. Only his spirit vision had convinced him to talk peace with the Unwanted Ones.

Kop shivered at the thought: Buka's vision had been wrong. Then he saw the spear. It had lost all of its red colour. It was tucked under the spreading branches of a large tree. Without a keen eye, he would have taken it for another branch. But its shaft, smooth with use, had caught his attention. With the spear in his hand, he walked back to the burial ground where Tehonee and Kuise were waiting. They did not like being alone at such a sacred time. Kop smeared the spear with the precious red mixture.

They carried the remains to the burial site and laid them in the graves. Tehonee wept. Kuise cried softly and was not chided for it. Kop laid Buka's great spear by the bones of his right hand. When all was done to Kop's liking, they covered the grounds with soil, stones, and boughs. Over it all they placed the sweet-scented branches from pine saplings, and without looking back, the three Beothuk left the burial ground.

Walking out from the forest and standing on the beach above the cove, they all heard the screech of the fish hawk. At first no one could see the bird. Suddenly, it was there, hovering above the sea as before. As Kop and his family watched, the magnificent bird dropped out of the sky toward the sea, like a thrown spear. They watched, and just before the bird entered the water, its body turned, curved talons pointed down and its wings canted back over its sleek body, its feathers bristling with speed. It entered the water claws first with a great splash. Its wings battered. Water glistened with the sun as the hawk rose. The bird screamed in triumph, and Kop shivered visibly. The hawk's cry was similar to Buka's triumphant call. The hawk beat its way out of the sea on battering pinions, and gripped in its talons was a shiny salmon struggling for a life that was already gone.

THE FAMILY MADE their way north by the coast for weeks. They spent the last days of autumn in the largest of bays filled with islands, where a great river bled into the sea. Following that estuary, and guided by the schools of salmon which milled around that river mouth every year, they entered the forest to their winter hunting grounds beyond. It was an age-old route proven true and profitable for ages. They gathered as much fish, dried and smoked and packed in light birchbark containers, as they could carry with them. Even Kuise was expected to carry as much as she could. And in all of that time, as they worked their way north and then west into the huge estuary, they saw no one. Twice they approached campgrounds known to them, but the *mamateeks* there were unused. The firepits were cold, and the drying racks were bare of fish. It was very disturbing to Tehonee.

"Where are the others, Kopituk? Why are they not here to

glean from the mighty river the shiny salmon which the Great Spirit guides into our weirs?" They stood talking in the trees directly opposite another *mamateek* from which no welcoming smoke was rising.

"I know not where they are, my woman. But this I know. They have been here! See at the base of the *mamateek*. There! One side of the hide door. Repairs have been made." Kop's eye had caught the bright new bark added to the structure.

"Stay here and do not show yourself," he ordered. And in a low crouch he crept over the green, untrodden grasses toward the *mamateek*. He carried his bow and a quiver of arrows slung across his shoulder, and in his hand was a pointed spear. Kop's body was as tense as stone. He was afraid of what he would find inside the camp. He remembered all too well what he had witnessed in the lodge at the cove of death.

He neared the door opening and crouched low, listening. He heard nothing from within. He knew he would not. There was no physical sign anywhere of the life he had hoped for. He noticed the tracks of field mice through the grass leading under the frame and into the camp. The birds above him chirped and twittered without fear. Shivering in anticipation, Kop pulled the hide door wide open. Light spilled inside, and after an eternity, he entered. With his hand trembling behind him, he kept the hide flap open. There was no one inside. His eyes soon adjusted to the wan light inside the cave-like shelter, and some of the tension left his body. It was obvious to Kop they had been here. New pine boughs had been added to the sleeping ledges. Rotting fish hung from a pole above the dead fire. The fish had been hung to be smoke-cured but had not been eaten. Nothing of any value was inside the camp, only a few tattered hides. The *mamateek* had been looted!

Kop stepped outside. He had a bad feeling in his stomach. He called to Tehonee. She had been anxiously waiting and came running toward him. Kuise was by her side.

"They were here, but only for a short time. The small sleek fish which come to the brooks in spring have been gathered and have rotted. Few have been eaten. Cowardly thieves have taken their belongings." He reported this to Tehonee with downcast eyes.

"Kopituk, tell me true this time. Are there bones inside to be buried?"

"No, Tehonee. There is nothing inside, living or dead."

Kuise ran around the encampment as Kop studied the grounds for more signs. Tehonee lifted the door covering and went inside. She let the hide fall behind her. In the semi-darkness, Tehonee's eyes searched around. Kop was right: they had been here in the spring, but not long after. Kop was right about something else, too. Thievery had taken place. To take something unattended and not guarded was accepted by her kind, but to steal from a functioning camp filled with the full pursuit of living was unacceptable and unheard of.

Opening the door and peering outside to make sure Kop was not coming, Tehonee crawled around the camp floor on her hands and knees. The sleeping pallets had been stitched with new pine boughs. The green colours were fading, but the boughs had not been pressed as they would have been had they been used. Tehonee pushed her hands under the boughs farthest from the firepit, in the centre of the *mamateek* and hard against the bark wall of the structure. She found what she was looking for right away.

It was a small rabbit-skin pouch cured to fine soft leather and tied at the mouth with a thin thong. Tehonee crept to the door again and peered out. She could hear Kuise playing down over the bank where a small stream flowed. Kop was walking around the perimeter with head down, searching for spoor. Seated with her back to the bark wall inside the shadowy *mamateek*, Tehonee opened the pouch and pushed her hand inside. She pulled out several swaths of soft rabbit fur without the hide and several handfuls of goose down. It had been carefully woven by a woman's hand to attend to her monthly moon bleedings. No woman would leave without it. Those who lived here had fled without warning or time to prepare. Tehonee placed the pouch back where she had found it and left the *mamateek*. As she exited, Kuise came running up over the bank with great excitement. "I have found a *tapooteek* in the bushes by the brook, my mother! But it is filled with holes and will not carry us on the water."

Kop heard his daughter's cry and joined her and her mother. Kuise led them to the bank of the fast-moving brook. The *tapooteek* was small, used by no more than two paddlers. Kop grasped it by the bow. The centre of the craft folded down when he pulled on it. The boat had been brutally damaged. It had been done intentionally. Its sides had suffered long lateral gashes. Its tender ribs had been broken, and it was beyond repair. Kop, who had studied the sign with great intent, told Tehonee that those who had lived here had fled. The looting and the insult to the boat had been done since then.

"The Unwanted Ones!" said Tehonee.

Kop said nothing. And because he did not, Tehonee knew he agreed with her.

"I have seen their sign all around. Footprints without moccasins which dig deep into the earth. When they last walked here, the ground was wet and soft. Their sign remains," Kop said.

Kuise was very excited to be a part of the investigation, but her father was not pleased.

"You should not have wandered away on your own, Small One! There may be danger all around us."

Kuise's small face fell. His stern look had taken the glory from his daughter's discovery. Bending down to her level, Kop said in a gentle voice, "But you have shown much courage. We will look more at the *tapooteek* only you have found." They had walked back up the bank as they talked. Kuise's face beamed again with pride, and back to the brook she ran, her parents following.

The *tapooteek*, what was left of it, had not been pulled ashore. It had been washed ashore by the waves inside the mouth of the brook which ran into the sea. With steely, knowing eyes, Kop studied it for signs. He knew they were there. He just had to find them. He instructed Tehonee to keep watch all around, especially to the open bay, while he searched for clues.

He found a birchbark bailer half filled with water floating upright inside the damaged *tapooteek*. Kop tasted the water from the bailer. Though fresh water from the brook was present in the boat, the water from the bailer tasted salty. Whatever had happened to the boat and those aboard had happened in the bay. What he had first mistaken for red ochre on the upper edges of the *tapooteek*, and showing everywhere above its waterline, was blood. It was not the thick, dark blood of seals or the bright, thin blood of fish. It was human blood!

The boat had been slashed vertically and laterally several times by something very sharp. There were a few small, perfectly round holes on one side of the *tapooteek*, but not on the opposite side. Kop had seen such holes before: in the dead bodies of the friends he had buried. He instinctively knew the wounds in the bodies, like the wounds in the *tapooteek*, were caused by the shiny black staffs of the Unwanted Ones. It was clear to Kop that the little band who lived here had fled in their boat without taking any of their belongings. It puzzled him for the longest time, for in times of danger, his kind would always retreat into the forest, where they could easily hide. He found the answer on the edge of the forest behind the *mamateek*.

The deep prints of boots had come from the forest. He backtracked. It took a while. The spoor was old and had been made long ago. But to one born of the forest, whose life depended upon his ability to read spoor, the signs were there. He just had to concentrate. The tracks he followed were not of woodsmen. They had left a trail of broken branches and heavy footprints which showed their direction of travel. They had walked parallel to the coast from the long point of the cove beyond the *mamateek*.

There the print of a heavy boat drawn above the tidemark was still visible in the cloying mud of the cove. Some of the men had waited by the boat. Their tracks, tramping around in the same place, as if impatient, were impacted, and though faded were still clear to Kop. In his eye, Kop knew what had been carried out here. It was a guerrilla tactic used by native peoples everywhere. The Unwanted Ones who had gone through the forest had rushed the *mamateek*, shouting and screaming, making great noise to frighten the family of Beothuk. It had worked all too well. The Beothuk had fled for their lives, paddling furiously out the cove and rounding the long point where the others were waiting, guns in hand.

Those in the *tapooteek* had all been killed or drowned, or had escaped with grave wounds. Kop was sure of it. He would search the shoreline for them. Though he would search diligently, he did not expect to find them.

"I will go with you, Kopituk," said Tehonee, her voice hopeful. "My eyes are sharp as the hawk who sits on her eggs, and my step is almost as light as yours. And Kuise will not delay us."

"No, Tehonee. The trail will be long and need feet as stealthy as *abideshook* the night cat and will demand my greatest skill. I will best do it alone. With Kuise, here you will stay and wait for my return. I will return after the second sleep." Kop's voice had taken the stern edge Tehonee knew so well not to argue with. She tried another ploy.

"What if the Unwanted Ones return, my hunter?"

"They have done the deed of the cowards and have taken all that is of value to them. Their way is one of senseless murder and greed. They will not return to ground already ravaged. Of this I feel sure."

With Tehonee and Kuise confined to a campsite well away from the *mamateek* and hidden among the trees, and with Tehonee instructed to use no cooking fire, Kop began his search. As he travelled, he seldom showed himself but kept to cover, all the while searching, hoping for some sign of his people. He knew those he sought would leave little trace of their passing. Their trail would not be as brazen as that of the Unwanted Ones. And because of this, and knowing after being attacked they would be even more cautious, he kept all the more alert. But after two nights of little sleep and days of fruitless search, he bent his way back to his family, who were waiting anxiously for his return. The sun was low in the sky on the fourth day when he neared the place where he had left them. Despite his search being a failure, he lengthened his step, eager to see his family.

10

TEHONEE HAD WATCHED with trepidation as Kop left on his quest. The wilderness was her home, and she feared little in it, but the events which had taken place this season on the coast caused her to fear a wilderness both strange and un-known to her. Her world was being invaded, and a change vile to her way of life was coming unchecked. Tehonee sensed this and would talk more of it to Kop, if he would allow it. From her earliest memory gathered around the campfires in-side the winter *mamateeks*, Tehonee had learned there may be others in the broad world apart from her own kind. The elders, seated at their place of honour closest to the fire and away from the smoke spiralling for the smoke hole above, had kept the ancient tales alive. Lying against the wall of the shelter in her warm robes of caribou, Tehonee had listened well, and she had remembered the fear she had felt at the telling of such tales. One tale in particular had stayed with her. She remembered snuggling closer to her patient mother, and when attempting to question her about what the seer was saying, she had been silenced with a stare from her mother's gentle eyes.

* * * * *

THE TELLER OF stories stood and huffed aloud, signifying the importance of what he was about to relate. The same elder had told the same tale many times, but each time he was paid heed as if it were the first telling. Tehonee looked through the grey smoke at the man, who shimmered and looked ghostly. The fire crackled and snopped and flicked shadows around the sides of the lodge. The seer had the attention of them all, and he began, his voice hypnotic.

One of their great Beothuk hunters, fearless and ever adventurous, had led his clan far to the north, the elder told them. They had ventured beyond the deep forests and up over the plateaus where the deer were beyond number. On they trekked, ever northward, guided by the stars, following the coast and skirting around mountains, through deep sylvan valleys, hunting and fishing as they journeyed. The hunters led them up over the last huge point of land, far to the north where the tuckamore grows. And all throughout their sojourn, the sea to their right hand, from which comes the morning sun, was endless; but on their left hand, where the sun carried away the light each day, a distant land appeared up over the lip of the sea, from where it was said people of their own skin colour lived. On they journeyed for many days: hunting, fishing, gathering, and exploring.

And then one bright day, hidden and peering among the dwarf spruce, the wanderers beheld a great panorama. The point of land over which they had travelled for weeks was at last swallowed up by the salt sea. And upon the grassy, undulating plain leading to the water's edge were men dressed in a strange garb. They all appeared to be big men. But as the Beothuk watched, children appeared. One of the newcomers, obviously a woman, held a child to her naked breast, white as snow. The adults were dressed from head to toe in what appeared to be leather hides braced and crossed with shiny lashings. The faces of all the men were covered with hair the colour of winter grasses and earth. The hair of one of the men was the colour of new snow, and he walked with a limp. Many of them, including the women and children, wore pointed headpieces which shone in the sunlight.

The activity of the strange people was centred on high mounds covered with green grass, into which they frequently entered and reappeared at will, without bending down. Partially drawn onto the beach below the mounds of earth were two boats which defied the Beothuk imagination. As they looked on in rapt wonder, another boat with even more wonders appeared around the point to the west. It flew before the waves as though a great spirit carried it before the wind. Flying obliquely above the centre of this huge boat was a billowing sail filled with a free wind.

As the boat neared, the sail with rectangular stripes of faded brown and dirty grey snapped and yawed at its holdings. Reaching high above the boat's prow was the carved figure of a strange beast with bared fangs. The boat came nearer. Men appeared, standing above its sides. Shouts came from the boat and were answered loudly from the land. The sail was dropped around the feet of the boatmen, and without further ado, the huge boat was run aground upon the shore. It listed over on its side, and those aboard—men, women, and children—jumped into the water and ran upon the shore, where they were greeted by the others. As the astonished Beothuk watched, strange animals were unceremoniously thrown over the sides of the boat. Then, bleating in fear, with their small, pointed heads and long, twitching ears barely above water, they floundered to shore, where they stood and shook the water from their thin sides. They looked like caribou fawns. Some of them even had stubs of antlers. Two of them had swollen teats hanging between their hind legs. While standing and looking all around at their new surroundings, they allowed their young to suckle.

But they were not deer. This the Beothuk knew. The Beothuk, still in hiding, stared until their eyes watered and their muscles cramped. Then they heard a loud yapping from below. It was followed by the appearance of a fox-like animal, which promptly hopped over the side of the boat and swam ashore with apparent delight. Standing on the beach, the animal shook itself violently. Droplets of sea water from its body flashed in the sunlight. The animal was not much bigger than a dog fox, but its hide was white with tawny wolf-like patches. With the water dislodged from its coat, the dog raced after the goats, barking and nipping at their heels. The animals pranced and cried and jumped to avoid its teeth. One of the men roared at the dog. With bowed head and drooping tail, it approached as if knowing what was to come. A long leg, booted in leather, smote the dog viciously in the ribs. Crying in pain, it sprang toward the woods. At the edge of the tangled trees, it suddenly stopped. Its cry of pain changed to one of discovery. It barked and yapped loudly, with its head pointed toward the woods. The man who had kicked the dog yelled at it again, but the dog stood its ground, barking and howling at the wondrous scent emanating from the empty woods.

The Beothuk had waited with drawn bow as the dog approached. The hunter could have easily killed the *mammass-mit*, which barked like a fox in the moonlight and howled like a lone wolf in heat. But fearing the alarm it would raise, he retreated instead. Well away and upwind from the camp of the strangers, the Beothuk prepared their campsite in a small valley by the side of a pond, where trout jumped after flies, ducks skittered, and the leads of fat hares made their way through the brambles.

The Beothuk returned the next day, and from a hiding place downwind of the dog, they kept a vigil and studied the strangers. The hunter who led the Beothuk was as stealthy as the black fox. Keeping under cover, he crept closer than the others. And that night at the campfire he told of all that he had seen close up.

He had watched in fascination the people whose face and hand skin were almost the colour of his own, yet their arms and necks, when he caught glimpses of them under their clothing, were the colour of birchbark. The women brought water to their cooking fires from a nearby stream in leather buckets similar to the ones the Beothuk used. But the black cauldrons hanging over the fire were like nothing he had ever seen. Dozens of seabirds, barely plucked and not cleaned, just as many fish and baskets of eggs, animal hearts and livers were dropped into them, all at the same time. And though the fire rose all around them, the great pots were not consumed. The mixed odours of the cooking food smelled good to he who watched. The goats ran free around the campsite and nibbled on the grasses. Two of them whose milk bladders were swollen tight bleated and stopped eating. Their teats were elongated and oozing milk.

A young woman with long, yellow hair and clad in a tight-fitting leather skirt, with a leather container swinging from her hand, ran toward the animals and herded them together. The goats were suddenly docile at the woman's approach and stood as if waiting. Dropping to her knees, the woman grabbed the nearest goat. Reaching under the animal's belly, she grasped two of its swollen brown teats, and milk came squirting into the leather vessel she had placed underneath. This continued for a time, until the first goat was freed and the second one endured the same indignity, seemingly without any dispute. Both animals bounded away and commenced eating again.

Then the woman who had drained the milk from the goats did another strange thing. Still on her haunches, she raised the leather container to her lips and drank the warm milk. Her thirst quenched, she wiped the corners of her mouth with one hand and stood up with the amphora of milk in the other hand. With her hips swaying and her sun-coloured hair bending in the wind, she walked back to one of the earthen mounds covered in green sods and disappeared inside.

All of this was a marvel to the Beothuk. But what their leader had to tell them next both upset and angered them. He said he was sure the dog had caught his scent and barked while looking his way. One of the men yelled at it, and the animal cowered away but kept yapping and looking toward the copse where the hunter lay hidden. The dog was always yapping.

Fish were spread and drying on every boulder up from the shoreline. Fish hung on racks above smoky pits. Seal skins and beaver and marten pelts were stretched on wooden frames to cure, and the remains of rotting seal carcasses were rank in the air. There was more. Pulled high up the beach was the huge carcass of a blunt-nosed whale. Men with long knives were cutting the rich blubber from its sides, revealing enough tender dark meat to feed an entire tribe. Whales were a dangerous animal to hunt from a *tapooteek*, and the Beothuk seldom managed to kill one.

All of the men carried bigger knives wrapped in sheaths hung from their sides. The knives were as broad and as long as a man's arm. Frequently they pulled the long knives out of their sheaths, spat on them, then rasped them again and again against boulders until they were honed. They tested the sharpness of the knives by wielding them against shrubs and grasses, which collapsed like waves on a beach. Deer hides, green and fatty, were scattered around, and hides already cured were stacked against the green shelters. Baskets of berries—red, yellow, and blue—were laid by. And haunches of deer were spitted and roasting over glowing charcoals.

When they who had observed all of these things on the shore and had finished telling all they had witnessed, it was quiet for a while. The campfire crackled, and flankers sprang into the air. A night bird crooned. The stars overhead beamed. Then a woman, who should not have spoken until a hunter had spoken first, exclaimed in a fearful voice:

"They are the Unwanted Ones, come among us, as foretold by the Mages." She was hushed by harsh stares and the stamping of feet and was shamed into silence. But she had opened up a train of thought. A man with greying hair, who had suffered much on the trail to get there, but who was allowed to come because he was wise in the old ways and far-seeing, spoke:

"It has been passed down from a thousand fire smokes by those who have long passed. That great *tapooteeks* were seen coming up out of the morning sea in summer. Flying over the green waves, carried by spreading wings which never beat, they landed on our northern shores. Strange men jumped out and roamed our shoreline. But that was a summer when the Great Spirit commanded winter to linger long. Plants did not bloom, berries died on the vine, and spawning fish stayed away from our shores. The Great Spirit, all-knowing, showed the strangers they were unwanted in our land, and after a time they left, disappearing down over the edge of the eastern sea from which they had come."

"If this is true, why has the Great Spirit not driven the Unwanted Ones from our shores once again?"

"You cannot question the Great Spirit! Who knows their ways? Even the Mages fear their wisdom."

"The Unwanted Ones are not True Men. Their faces are

covered with hair, and like rats they sleep in burrows beneath the earth."

"Enough about spirits and men with faces covered with hair. They have taken the fruit from our fields and meat and furs from our land without permission. Put arrows into their chests. Take back what they have stolen from us. Drive them back into the sea from which they came. The will of the Great Spirit is with us."

"This is true. The Unwanted Ones came up out of the sea like a huge *si'kane'su*. They came from a place known only to the Great Spirit, who keeps the endless sea in trust for all peoples. But this is our land. They kill our deer and trap for our warm furs without asking. And I, too, have seen the dens where they dwell. We must drive them back until they fall over the edge of the earth again."

THE TALK WENT on until the fire died and the night grew cold. But before the dawn heralded a sleepless night, a decision had been reached. The Beothuk would attempt to drive the Vikings from their shores.

The Norse were a fearless breed of people, men and women who waged war as a means of conquering. On fields of battle, their yells alone were enough to paralyze their foe. Flashing swords, halberds, and heavy maces were their weapons. On open meadows of battle, even outflanked and outnumbered, they were undaunted and seldom lost a fight.

But they feared the dark, trackless forests unknown to them and ventured there only in groups, to trap the nearby ponds and brooks or to hunt deer on the open barrens. They never entered the forest at night, and never alone. It was their only weakness. They knew nothing of guerrilla fighting. The Indians of North America invented it.

The first night, the Beothuk killed the dog with a long arrow fluted deep into its chest. The next night it rained, and sounds were muted. Silent as the wolf, and with no dog to raise the alarm, the Beothuk crawled up over the grassy roofs, below which the Vikings snored loudly, and stuffed plaits of wet bog into the smoke holes. When they were forced out of their earthen hovels into the black night, two of them were struck down with arrows. And when the dreary dawn came, they discovered their goats were missing. The Unwanted Ones ran to the edge of the forest and roared their anger in a strange tongue. Their women screamed as loudly and kept yelling over and over: "Skraelings! Skraelings!" And for the first time, they showed signs of fear.

All that season the Beothuk kept up their assaults. They hid low by the trails and stabbed at the legs of the Vikings as they walked by, causing great wounds. Swifter than deer, the Beothuk bounded away like shadows into the forest. They were sometimes followed with shouts of anger, for only short distances, until, finding no sign of their attackers and fearing to lose their way, the Vikings retreated. Their wounded, whom had walked in on their own feet, now had to be carried out by others. They would also need the prolonged care of others. It weakened their defences. Though they killed and harried the Vikings, never did the Beothuk molest their young or their women.

But the Vikings were not afraid to fight. They thrived in open battle and proudly bore the scars. One day the Beothuk, triumphant after their sneaking forays and with lowered guard, were caught in the open. Four of them were fiercely slain in the skirmish by the Vikings' swords, which nearly cleaved them in half. And a young girl in her first year of bleeding was carried away. Two of the Vikings were killed with spear and arrows, and many more had been wounded with a flurry of arrows. The ground was red with blood.

It was two weeks later before the Beothuk returned to continue their attacks. From the cover of the trees they watched the Vikings load their boats. A tall, wild-haired woman screaming, "Skraeling!" came out from one of the shelters and dragged the bound Beothuk maiden behind her. She hurried toward the waiting boats. The captive girl had been beaten. Her clothing was torn, she looked dishevelled and terrified, and she was bleeding. Knowing she was to be carried aboard the dreaded winged boats, the girl screamed piteously and kicked at her captor. One of the men near her smote the girl a long-handed blow on the head with a gnarled stick. She slumped to the ground.

Her attacker grabbed her by her hands and dragged her behind him to the beach. He was followed by the white woman, who was looking nervously behind her. The man waded waist deep in the water, still dragging the unconscious Beothuk girl. The icy water appeared to rouse her, and she tried to stagger to her feet. Her head was bleeding. Crying and pleading for help from the ones she knew were watching from the woods, the maiden was dragged over the side of the boat. Under a rain of blows, she was silenced again. The men pushed the boats from the shore with long poles, and the vessels' wings were hauled aloft. The wings caught and held the wind, and the boats carried the Unwanted Ones away from the land. Once, from a distance, the despairing cry of the captive maiden, who had all of her birthing years ahead of her, came to the shore. And the Skraelings, emerging from the forest, made their way toward the deserted grassy mounds.

11

TEHONEE SHIVERED AT the memory of the legend handed down by her people. She knew Kop had heard the story as often as she had. But until this season on the coast, he had paid it little heed. Now he had been gone a long time. She wondered if his search would be rewarded. She had a bad feeling in her stomach. Tehonee knew that, although they came in different, bigger boats carried on many wings, they were still the Unwanted Ones. And their numbers were far greater.

Her bad feelings were further steeped by her musings about the legends handed down. With Kopituk gone, her only comfort was her daughter, Kuise. She looked all around. Kuise was nowhere to be seen. She called her name, thinking the child had gone into the woods to relieve herself. There was no response. Then with a sinking feeling, she remembered Kuise had asked to go back to the ravaged campsite. She had told her no, she was never to return there alone. Tehonee broke into a run, knowing as only mothers do where Kuise was. She had disobeyed her mother's direct command and had returned to the campsite. Tehonee knew why. Kuise had spied a carved toy in the bushes at the campsite and wanted to take it. Her father, unsure if its owner was dead—

and if so, then the toy should be buried with the body—had told her no.

Angry at her daughter's disobedience, Tehonee quickened her step. She saw Kuise seated outside the deserted *mamateek*, playing with the toy she had returned for. Tehonee's anger melted. She would not tell Kop about this. She was about to call her daughter, but then she saw them. Four of the Unwanted Ones were drawing a longboat upon the beach below where her daughter was sitting. She was further astonished to see the one with the red hair among them, so well described by Kop. Kop was wrong. They had returned! With a cry of desperation, she ran toward her daughter.

"Run into the forest, Kuise! Run! Run like the wind and don't look back!"

Kuise was alarmed as much by her mother's sudden appearance as by her cry of warning. She sprinted for the trees, taking the toy with her, and was quickly out of sight.

At Tehonee's cry, the men looked up in surprise. They had not expected the site to be occupied again. Guns appeared in their hands. Tehonee saw them and remembered Kop's words: *When they raised the long staffs to their shoulders, thunder and fire spewed out and Buka fell dead.* The guns were drawn to their shoulders. Tehonee ran to them, ripped open her bodice, and exposed her breasts.

"I am woman!" she shouted.

She was still shouting when the first shot tore into her naked breast. She looked down at her chest in disbelief. It was as if she had just been speared, but she had seen no spear thrown. Only a flash of fire, accompanied by the sudden thunder-like slap. Unbearable pain filled her chest. It was followed by a wave of extreme nausea and a weakness so intense her eyes were closing. Directly in her view, and bursting in

fury out of the forest, was what she thought was an apparition. She forced her eyes wide open. It was Kopituk running
toward her. His long, black hair was flowing behind him. His
lean, red face, though clenched in fury, was wondrous to look
upon. His bow jumped in his hand, and his great cry of defiance was beautiful to hear. Her great hunter had returned, as
he had said he would. All would be well. Then the second shot
entered her breast, just below the first one. Tehonee's vision of
Kop faded, and with her eyes still open, she crumpled to the
ground.

KOP HAD ALREADY broken into the long stride of the home-
ward-bound hunter when the first cries erupted out of the
wilderness ahead of him. It was high-pitched and pleading.
It came again, and he recognized the words as well as the
voice.

*Run into the forest, Kuise! Run! Run like the wind and don't
look behind!*

It was Tehonee's cry for her daughter to flee from some
terrible danger. Kop bolted forward, as fleet as a deer. Then
came the same crack he had heard from the men carrying the
staffs outside the *mamateeks* at the cove of death. It was followed by another anguished cry from Tehonee.

I am woman!

Her cries were silenced by a shot and were replaced by
calls and laughter shouted in a foreign tongue. They shot into
the forest in the direction of the fleeing Kuise. Kop sprang out
of the forest like an enraged animal. From his throat thundered
a cry to put Buka's hunting cry to shame. Two men were standing near a boat whose bows were barely touching the beach,
and two more were standing over the still body of Tehonee.
She was lying on her back, and her deerskin tunic was bloody.

Kuise was nowhere to be seen. Surely they had not killed an innocent child.

The men standing above Tehonee stared in surprise at the fury racing toward them. One of them had turned to face him, when a short arrow fletched with hawk feathers entered his throat. He dropped the long-barrelled musket and fell to his knees, clutching at the arrow. Blood poured from between his clawing fingers, and he gagged before he fell down next to Tehonee.

The man next to him was the red-haired man with the blotchy red skin. He was fumbling to load his empty gun, which was still smoking in his hands, when Kop's second arrow, shot on the run, penetrated his right side all the way to his hip bone. The man screamed in pain and fear, dropped the gun, and limped toward the boat. The arrow protruding from his ripped clothing oozed blood. Two shots rang out from the men standing by the boat. Kop fell to his knees beside Tehonee. His sudden drop to see to his wife saved his life as the lead balls whizzed over his head. He saw in an instant she was dead. It angered him beyond all reason, and he jumped to his feet again, his cry of revenge more terrible than before. At a shout from the red-haired man scrambling to board the boat, the men stopped reloading their weapons and pushed the boat into deeper water.

They dragged the wounded man over the gunnel. Grabbing for the oars and pulling hard, they shot away from the beach. Kop was running along the water's edge when he let loose another arrow, which thunked into the hull of the boat, just below the red-haired man. Waist deep in water, he stopped and drew his bowstring to his chin. He let it go. Another cry came from the red-haired man. Kop's arrow had cut through his cheek, but it was only a flesh wound and had not killed him. Kop regretted not using his long arrow. He had aimed for the throat, and a long arrow would have found its mark.

Realizing they were out of range of the Beothuk's arrows, the men in the boat stopped to return fire with their own weapons. They were reaching for their guns when a roar from their wounded companion started them rowing again, and they pulled away with haste. Kop found a long arrow. Aiming carefully, he let loose. It soared high, straight and true, but fell short of the moving boat. Kop screamed his anger and grief after the Unwanted Ones.

"Killers of women and small ones! Cowards! Eaters of maggots! Vermin!" And then, what was for him the vilest of insults, he bellowed after them, "Your brother, who you have left behind, will never enter the spirit world!"

Weakened by his frantic run through the forest, the fighting, and the shock of seeing his woman dead before him, Kop staggered. He half ran, half crawled ashore, creating great splashes of water around him. Maybe he was wrong! It had all happened so fast. Tehonee was not dead, just wounded.

Still grasping the bow, he ran in a headlong fumble up the beach and into the clearing to fall down across the body of his beloved Tehonee. Pulling her into his arms, shaking her, and staring into her open eyes, he shouted her name over and over again. Tehonee was still warm, but she was dead. Tears poured from his eyes. His throat muscles constricted. He gasped for air and laid Tehonee's body down, with her beautiful face looking up at him. Her clothing was open. Her firm, round breasts were naked and stained with blood. She had bared her breasts to show the Unwanted Ones she was woman, but in vain. They had killed her anyway. From deep in his soul, a pitiful cry poured out of Kop. It was the sound of despair, of a beast broken and defeated.

It carried far enough to reach Kuise, who had run into the forest as ordered, but who had come back and was now peering out. For the first time in her life, she saw her father's tears. Kuise's own cry of misery came as loud and unstoppable as waves rushing upon a rocky beach. She threw the branches of her hiding place aside and ran to her mother, falling down by her side. The child sobbed uncontrollably, pressing her cheek against her mother's.

Kopituk carried Tehonee's body from the clearing and placed it under the trees while Kuise looked on. He grabbed the guns by the barrel, one at a time, and with all of his strength, backed by anger and frustration, he rapped them against the trunk of a tree until their long barrels were bent and the wooden stocks were shattered and useless.

Then Kop began a gruesome task. He did so methodically and without haste. On his haunches, he stripped the dead man of his clothing until he was naked. The man's skin was white and pasty. He stank so badly of sweat and filth, Kop retched before he continued. He turned the naked man until his head was facing the forest, where he knew his spirit did not want to go.

Kuise, still on her knees and sobbing beside her dead mother, watched her father. Halfway between the white man's chin and shoulder, Kop cut the man's neck all the way around, right to the spine. Blood poured out. Bending the head back with one hand, he made two vicious chops with his knife to the man's vertebrae before the spine broke, completely severing the head from the body. The dead man's face and head were covered with brown, matted hair unused to water. He had died with his eyes closed. Kop cut the eyelids, making sure the eyes would be forever open. Turning the man face down, he cut deep between his spread legs until blood and his ruptured bowels poured out on the ground. The smell was nause-ating and fouled the air all around. Taking the severed head, he pushed it face first into the cavity. Unable to take the smell any longer, Kop stood and kicked the hated man's head as far as he could into the man's own putrid innards. He had taken his revenge on one of his wife's killers. But his revenge would not be complete until the head of the man with the red hair was displayed on a stake.

KOP CARRIED THE body of his beloved Tehonee first in his arms, and as she stiffened, on his back for two days. Behind him trudged the dazed Kuise, her small shoulders heavy with bur-den. It had taken the best part of the day for Kopituk to console the child. He allowed her a time of grieving, but in the end, he had to pull his anguished daughter away from Tehonee's stiff-ening form. It was then Kop saw the small round hole in the waist of Kuise's dress and knew it for what it was. They had tried to kill his child along with her mother!

Kop's face was a mask of pain, sorrow, and above all, hate. He had never known such hatred. He could only speak to Kuise with garbled instructions as they went along.

If the killers had fled through the forest, he would find them no matter how well they tried to hide their trace. But the killers had fled over the water, where no trace was ever left be-hind. No matter. When he found others of his kind, he would leave Kuise in their care. Then he would return and soothe his soul with the sweet purge of revenge.

Far away from the place where she had been brutally mur-dered, Kop laboriously carried the body of the only woman he had ever loved. He reached the place he sought and lowered her body down. The place Kop had chosen to bury his woman had been an intuitive choice. It was a secreted valley, well up from the coast, where a clear brook meandered through grit and soil. Where the water continued out of the dark forest into the bay, its mouth was a mere step wide and easily overlooked as a waterway of any significance. Long ago, Kop had discovered it while searching for eels. The brook's arrival into the bay belied its course, for beyond its merging with the sea and away from the saltwater shrubs, its narrow, rocky indraft widened into a shallow stream flowing merrily from a long pond nestled among the wooded hills. Where the brook left the pond there was a natural, flat meadow of lush grasses. It had been created by countless spring floods bringing deposits of nutrients. Tall aspens and stately white birches rustled in the wind. They were backed by a sloping ridge of pine and fir. It was a place of grandeur and solitude. More than that, it was the place where Kopituk and Tehonee had consummated their first act of love. Kop remembered the place well. He had bedded Tehonee many times in many different places after that. On warm beaches by the sounding sea on moonlit nights; on sweet-smelling grasses by the side of a lapping lake in full daylight; and beneath robes of fur blankets they had explored the ways of one flesh and shared their young love.

But in their winter house, that same season, when Tehonee's time of bleeding had not come and her soft brown belly swelled with life, she had told Kop the life within her had been conceived in the place of their first loving. And Kop, who knew nothing of the mysterious ways of women, believed her. It came to him now, as he laid his burden down, that here in this place, where he and Tehonee had lavished in love and merged their seed into blessed life, he would, in death, lay down the mother of that life. He glanced at Kuise, who was struggling to get the pack from her shoulders.

The walk had eased her sorrow some. She staggered as

the weight of the load left her thin shoulders. The child was exhausted. Keeping up with her father had taxed her growing limbs. Her father had not spoken to her during the trek. Kuise wondered if he knew that it was she who was the cause of her mother's death. Her burden numbed her with guilt.

Kop cut fine inner bark from the white birch trees surrounding the campsite. He stained Tehonee's body and all of her belongings with red ochre, and she was prepared for burial. She was wrapped with the birchbark, and it was also anointed with the sacred stain. The purging was done, and Tehonee's body was laid down in the crypt beneath the moving trees. It was the second time in the space of one moon Kop was doing the burial ceremony, this one in silence. He flushed the smoke from the smouldering herbs all around Tehonee's gravesite, purifying it and preparing her for her sacred afterlife.

Kop and Kuise talked little. Kop allowed his daughter to help cover her mother's body with clean stones from the stream and to take part in the ceremony. She placed her mother's personal objects beside her in the grave: the thong Tehonee wore around her neck, braided with the fine neck hair of a deer fawn, and interlaced with tiny seashells; a small leather pouch of soft rabbit fur filled with goose down, which Tehonee had carried for her menses; and a birchbark basket wonderfully embroidered with bright feathers and a string of black kelp, filled with bone awls and needles and leather and spruce root thread for sewing. Kuise placed the latter by her mother's right hand, ready for her to use in the spirit world.

When Kop, on his knees above the grave, began a low, deliberate chanting which called the spirits to come all around, Kuise shivered and was afraid. Her father gave her no comfort. He shed no tears. His face was like stone. Even the songbirds had quieted while Kop delivered his dirge to the four winds.

He rose to his feet and motioned with his hand for Kuise to rise also, when the cries began on the pond. Both father and daughter turned toward the sound. It was the mournful cry of the male loon calling as the light faded. As they listened, the bird called once more, long and sorrowing. Then, distinct on the still air, came the pattering sound of the bird leaving the water. The hunter of fish cleared the trees. Then, emitting a magnificent requiem from its fluttering throat, the bird that mated for life flew away. Its cry faded away on the evening air. But no mate flew behind it.

12

THE NEXT MORNING, with the sun not even one-hand above the glow of the eastern sky, Kop and Kuise abandoned their camp and turned west into the bay splayed with islands, into which the great mother of all rivers poured. Here he would surely find some of his own people. Kuise would be welcome to stay with them, and Kop would return to avenge his wife's killing.

Kop and Kuise foraged for food in the bottom of coves, where their tidal pools had been drained by the ebb tides. Snails stuck to boulders, clams dug out of the sand, and mussels in blue beds provided for them. Kuise played with the small, eel-like tansies in her hands and gingerly carried crab to the waiting fire, where they were placed on hot rocks above their cooking fire and held with a stick until their struggles ceased. In the bottom of many muddy coves were squid by the thousands. Beached and stranded on the shore by the receding tide, the squid were dead or dying and easily gathered. Their skins, pulsating in death throes, were a constant change of colour: iridescent green, blue, red, and finally a pallid white. Their boneless flesh was tasty, filling, and easy to cook over an open fire. Their thin white flesh, once cleaned, and spread on rocks, dried in the hot sun and hardened to a tough jerky. Squid were used extensively and chewed for energy while on the trail.

Kop caught eels with his hands in the streams entering the bay. For this he used the finger grip well practised by his people, from which few eels ever escaped. Eels were prized as much for their elongated skins as they were for their tasty, oily flesh. The tough skins, well cured, had many uses, including for sewing and mending. But now Kop discarded the eel skins. He was neither a mender of rags nor a sewer of clothing. He was a hunter. Kop had taken to eating most of his food raw, and he cooked food more for Kuise than for himself. He was becoming bitter, and not finding more of his kind only angered him more.

On the outer edge of one point of land known to Kop, where a forest fire had burned to the water's edge a few years earlier, they feasted on blueberries. The bushes were so heavily laden with the sweet fruit, their branches bulged downwards. There were fields of berries stretching in a blue cast through the white skeletons of trees downed and those still standing. Father and daughter ate until their stool was skittered and blue before moving on.

Kop expected to find a Beothuk encampment over every point of land and by the side of each stream mouth. In many places he found where his people had been. *Mamateeks* and *meoticks* badly in need of repair had not been repaired this season. Rock weirs built in the brooks by the Beothuk, their rock walls overturned by winter ice and spring floods, had not been corrected. No canoe for fishing, or *tapooteek* used to gather eggs from the offshore islands, were ever seen. On they went into the bay much loved by the Beothuk. Trees were resplendent with autumn colour. Leaves were falling. The nights were colder. The air had that harvest smell loved by all hunters. Schools of spawn-filled salmon waited at the end of this arm of water.

When they arrived at its wide mouth days later, weary with travel and forlorn with loss, they heard much shouting and excited commotion ahead of them. At first Kop picked up the pace, eager to meet friends. But all too quickly he signalled Kuise to the ground while he stole ahead once more to investigate.

Peering out from the trees, he looked in disbelief at the scene before him. Far out the bay, and with lines from their bows holding them there, were not one but two ships. The sails that had brought them here were furled. Their poles were naked and tangled with lines. Near the shore and in Kop's view were many smaller boats. In one of them, men were hauling a net filled with glistening salmon in over its canted gunnels. More salmon than Kop had ever seen caught at one time. The men shouted and called to each other in a language he could not understand. Many of the salmon were as long as Kop's arm. Those were instantly killed by a blow from a wooden mallet in the hands of the Unwanted Ones. Other, smaller salmon were untangled from the net and thrown carelessly into the bottom of the boat. The boat gunnels ran red with blood and shiny scales.

Gulls wheeled all around the boats, screeching for scraps of food. The trees above Kop's head rustled and sighed, shedding their leaves, as low bushes all around shivered and bent lazily in the breeze. Small birds sang and called. A raven, perched on a tree, croaked and clucked as it watched the activity in the bay. A searching crow flying by spotted Kop in hiding and suddenly veered from its intended course. He crouched to the ground, fearing the Unwanted Ones had noticed the sudden change in the bird's flight.

But the fishermen took no notice. They were bent on the slaughter of salmon they were pulling from the sea without end. They were landing so many fish, Kop feared the sea would be emptied. The men gathering the salmon were the Unwanted

Ones, but two of them were different. Their skin was the colour of Kop's, without the red paint. One of them wore buckskin. The other was dressed like the Unwanted Ones. They were the only ones among the group whose faces were hairless. The others were bearded. Kop's pulse raced as he stared, searching for the man with the red beard, but he was not among them. The two who appeared to be Indian did not work at the fishing but acted as guides, pointing to different places in the cove. Kop had seen them before, but farther inland, past the edge of the Beothuks' traditional hunting and trapping grounds. They were known to be another race of Indian who had travelled here over the great salt sea to the west and were called Mi'kmaq. The white men were obviously making great use of the two. Under their direction, they pulled the nets aboard and headed farther into the mouth of the river.

All around the shore were the signs of his people having fished for generations. Kop had fished here many times with his own family. Even Kuise knew the coves and runs in the river where the weirs had been built by Beothuk hands. She, too, had played her role in that fishery: running and splashing down the shallow runs, she had crowded the frightened salmon into the waiting traps, where the adults waited with their spears in hand. Now there was no fresh sign of any of his kind. Hungry, and confused by all he had witnessed, Kop made his way back to where Kuise was waiting for him. When she asked when they could go and visit the others, he merely growled in reply and ordered her to follow him. He led her away from the river and up through the forest, where majestic pine trees grew on the side of a hill. There he made camp for the night, and he and his daughter chewed tough strips of squid for their meal.

Kop watched the foreigners fish the estuary for salmon for

three more days. Their greed knew no bounds. The next day, he decided to seek out their night camp. He told Kuise she was to remain in camp and that he would return before the rising sun.

"You must not disobey, Small One. There is much danger all around us. Keep hidden," Kop told her firmly.

"I will not disobey my *ewinon*. I will remain here and say many *se'kos* for your safe return," Kuise answered, her head bowed. She wanted to tell her father her mother had been slain because she hadn't stayed at the camp, but she was afraid. Disobedience from one as young as Kuise meant severe punishment. She also wished she could hug him, as she had her mother. She had seldom been hugged by her father. When she raised her head again, Kop had already gone and she was alone.

KOP STARED OUT at the strange men from the copse of dense woods. He found their camp easily. Thick smoke was rising above the trees from several fires rising in a sheltered cove. They had built log structures there, the seams chinched tight with yellow moss.

Most of the men had ugly hair on their faces, and he could smell them from his hiding place. Their heads were covered with shapeless garments that hung below their ears and partially hid their hair. This tangled mess that grew to their shoulders was of different colours and not at all like the True Men. Most of the strangers' hair was the colour of dead grass, while some was almost white. Still more had dark hair, but none were totally black. Then he saw him. The one with the red hair. Kop's stomach quivered in anger. His jaw muscles tensed and he clenched his teeth. It took all of his resolve to stay in hiding while his heart pumped for revenge. But with so many against him, he was the one who would be killed, and with his death, Kuise's young life would never age.

He stared at the redhead the most. The red blotches on his face looked like sores. With satisfaction, Kop saw that the man was limping badly, and across his cheek he bore the deep, burning scar from his arrow. Many of the others also grew hair which covered their faces, but none of them resembled the ochre colour of the man with the red beard.

Their boats were drawn close to the rocky shore and fastened to the land with long, braided strands the likes of which Kop had never seen before. The boats themselves were not made of bark but of wood. The newcomers were full of mystery. They used tools strange to the watching Beothuk and carried themselves with an arrogant and careless demeanour. They were occupying Beothuk land without permission and yet posted no guard, nor for the most part showed any concern for their thieving acts. They acted as if they owned the land. Countless fish drying in the sun were laid across every available boulder and rock. Drying racks topped with boughs built above the ground bulged with fish curing in the sun. Blackflies crawled all over them and swarmed and buzzed above them.

Only one among them was beardless and carried himself differently. His eyes scanned the woods, and once his gaze fell across the low clump of trees where the red man lay hidden. But he saw nothing and returned to the group. Kop stared long at this tall, lean white man and decided that he would be the one to watch most carefully.

He crept closer, to a better vantage point. Holding himself motionless, he watched and waited. He, too, had listened all his life to the legends told down through the long years of the ancient Unwanted Ones. He was in full control of his emotions now, and remembering the old tales, he knew what he was going to do. He knew the guerrilla way. He would make the legend come alive again.

Presently, one of the heavy-clothed men emerged from the log structure. The solid wood opening he stepped through squealed with his appearance, and then he closed the door behind him. This man was almost as tall as the observant one, and though he wore a long, grizzly beard, he resembled the other beardless one, especially in his confident demeanour. At a rough command from this man, one of the others walked to the shoreline and out over a short, lungered bridge, where the boat bobbed on its mooring. Leaning back against the rope, he pulled the vessel close to the rocks and jumped aboard. The hunter was amazed to see the boat had barely moved.

Bending below the gunnels of the boat, the white man stood again, holding a large fish in each hand. He threw them onto the wharf. Again and again he repeated the work, now using a long-handled staff with a pointed, curved end. He pronged the fish onto the log surface, sometimes two and three at a time. As the hunter watched, his mouth watered for the delicious *bobusowet* which lay before him. Never before had he seen so many of the tasty white fish at one time.

After the boat was emptied, the fisherman joined the others on the shore. Now the work of cleaning the cod began in earnest. There was a small, rectangular table made of round logs, and onto this the slippery fish were placed one by one. Using a long, shiny knife, one of the white men eviscerated the cod and pulled the pinkish twin livers from the fish, then threw them into a puncheon nearby. The smell of the fermenting livers in the barrel was stirred anew with each addition.

A shorter man, his face hidden by a nest of dirty hair, seized the gutted cod and placed his left hand on the open breast of the fish. He placed his right hand on the head of the fish, and with two fingers poked into the eye sockets, he gave a violent wrench, one hand against the other, and the cod's head was removed against the sharpened edge of the table and thrown back into the water. Here the raucous seagulls swooped and dipped and fought over the discarded offal, their cries filling the cove as they feasted.

The tall, clean-faced man now grasped the fish and, using a shorter, slightly curved knife, removed the long backbone in three clean sweeps of his blade. Kop looked on. More than anything else he was seeing, the Beothuk was fascinated with the knives and their unbelievable sharpness.

FOR MORE THAN an hour he watched these strange men clean the huge catch of fish. When they'd finished and had thrown all the entrails into the sea at their feet, the bottom was covered with offal. They removed the fish from large wooden vats glistening with sea water. As Kop watched, the men carried layers of the split cod into a nearby lean-to with a slanted roof and three walls. From his position he could see inside the crude structure, for it was hard by the trees and close to his hiding place. Placing the fish on the brush-covered floor, one of the men brought forth buckets of a white, sandy substance from a smaller barrel inside, which he proceeded to toss over the spread cod. Their rough voices came to Kop, some of them high-pitched and others deep and growly, not at all resembling the language of the True People.

Why would these men in heavy clothes do such a thing? To carelessly catch and clean more cod than he had ever seen in one place, more than they could eat, only to cover them with coarse white sand? The cod his people managed to get were hung over the smoke fires and cured to a golden brown. Looking at the gulls screaming and feeding on the guts of the fish, his mouth watered for all the sweet-tasting cod hearts the white men had discarded. They were a sure delicacy among his people and were best eaten raw, fresh out of the fish. Kop suddenly thought of Kuise. She loved the fresh hearts. Unlike her father, it was the only thing Kuise would eat raw.

Once the fresh fish was cleaned and stored, the white men began another task. They gathered all of the drying fish in their arms and carried it aboard the boat. There were so many dried fish, it took many armloads before the rocks and drying racks were bare.

When they were finished, they strode away from their fish-cleaning place and left their shiny knives behind, stuck in the wooden table. He couldn't believe that such treasures would be left unguarded. His own knife never left his side, and he was always conscious of it.

THE NIGHT CAME creeping in from the grey sea and over the still bay, until the land across the quiet cove was black with only a faint glow left on the water. Waves sighed and chuckled around the rocks. The stars appeared, and still the red man waited. The noises inside the log dwellings where the strangers had gone finally quieted. A small light was dimmed until it gave no useful light at all, and heavy snores followed it out through the chinks of the tilts.

Leaving his cramped hiding place, Kop ran along the beach near the water's edge and stayed bent over until he came to the wharf. His moccasin-clad feet made only a rustling sound which blended with that of the waves meeting the land. Stopping once, he watched the remains of the cod entrails sway back and forth with the tide. Small splashes broke the water surface as unseen night fishes feasted on the offal. No sound came from the sleeping strangers save for the muffled snores. Kop's muscles had relaxed with the short sprint, and he sprung up onto the log deck in a graceful bound, landing on the balls of his feet like a lynx. He approached the table, reached up over the edge, and with both hands pulled the two shiny knives from the wood. He couldn't believe it had been so easy. The feel of the knives in his hands fascinated him. He instinctively knew their worth. Holding them by their smooth, wooden handles, he crept in over the lungered wharf until he was once again on the land. He was now very close to where the white men slept without a guard.

The smell of the stacked fish in the nearby enclosure beckoned to him. He paused outside it and forced himself to listen again. The night was still. The men slept on.

Reaching the tier of stacked codfish, he almost retched at the strong smell, but his curiosity prevailed. Reaching down, he grasped two of the fish by the tails and pulled them free of their briny bed.

Kop ran back over the wharf, both knives gripped firmly in his right hand and the white-coated cod in his left. He stopped at the wharf edge where the boat was tied. He wanted desperately to board the vessel. Looking back over his shoulder again, he listened for as long as three breaths. There were only the sounds of the forest night. He stepped aboard the boat as he had seen the others do. He was shocked that the vessel hardly moved at all under his weight. His eyes, well accustomed to the darkness, saw lying down on the boat's deck what he knew was one of the "wings" which carried the boat over the wide sea. He pulled at the edge of it, but it was tied in many places with ropes. It was time to test the sharpness of the knives he had taken. With deft movements, he slashed the sails until he had cut away a large portion. He placed the two fish on the cloth and rolled them into a bundle for carrying. It was heavier than he had expected, but he stepped out of the boat with it on his shoulder and used one of the knives again.

With one single draw, the painter holding the boat parted. Released from its tether, it swung away from the land. Kop was amazed by the ease with which he had cut the line.

He pounced down to the shingled beach. In his haste and elation, he made a slight noise. He froze, looking toward the tilts. The snoring continued. No one had heard him. The tide was leaving the cove and was taking the boat with it. Kop walked away from the landwash.

When he'd cleared the beach without any sign of detection and had gone several minutes into the shrouded forest, he stopped to inspect his good fortune. He passed the knives hand to hand, their balance and feel a pure joy to his hunter's soul. He marvelled at their construction. He had never seen such material before. He tested them against the tree bark and peeled the rough spruce rind effortlessly. He could only imagine how easily he would be able to clean an animal with such a tool.

Very pleased with his good fortune, he now turned his attention to the codfish. Peering at it in the darkness, he tore a strip from the thick breast of the fish and pushed a piece into his mouth. For a second he was puzzled. The unexpected taste exploded in his mouth. He retched again and again, trying to shake the putrid taste from his mouth. He pulled several small leaves from the bushes and crushed them in his hands, then stuffed them into his mouth and chewed them to a pulp before spitting them away. It took most of the foul taste with it.

Recovering from the vile taste, he threw the fish away into the night, where it fell with a soft thud upon the ground. Walking on into the darkness and still trying to rid his mouth of the terrible taste, he suddenly realized what it was—it tasted like sea water, of that he was sure. But what manner of magic was this? How could the strangers make the fish taste like sea water with the foul-tasting white sand? And why had they covered the codfish with it? Kop had no answers for such mysteries.

One thing was sure in his mind. If the strangers who were taking over his land were as unconcerned about their valuables as to leave them unguarded, then he looked forward to returning. Kop's mind whirled with strange thoughts. Then, exhausted by the day's events, he crawled under the branches of a fragrant fir tree and fell asleep.

EARLY THE NEXT morning, the red-haired man was the first to exit the tilts. His bladder was bursting. He hurried to the edge of the woods and urinated. When the door squeaked behind him, seagulls on the wharf squawked in fright and flew away. He looked at the birds and was turning to button his breeks before he realized the boat wasn't tied to the wharf. His cries of alarm brought the others running. The one whose face was bare ran out over the wharf. His pounding feet made the lungers bend. Reaching the wharf edge, he saw the painter knot still tied to the grump. It had not come untied. The standing part of the painter had been cut. One of the others shouted to him that their knives were gone. The men shouted, and with loaded muskets, they scoured the shoreline. They found no tracks other than their own, and they didn't enter the woods to look there. They found the boat farther out the bay. It had been broached on the rocks, most of its sail had been cut away, and it was half filled with water.

13

WHEN KOP RETURNED to camp that morning, Kuise was already awake and waiting. He ignored the concern in his daughter's eyes and told her to break camp. They were leaving. They prepared a new campsite not far away and still with easy access to the shore. They cooked over a small, smokeless fire. And that evening, with the new moon cradled in the arms of the old one and rising slowly above the treetops, young Kuise could bear her terrible burden no more:

"I went back to the deserted *mamateek* for the toy I saw there, my *ewinon*. While my mother was preparing the sleeping robes over the soft fir boughs and wasn't looking. The toy was the head of the hawk which hunts the sparrow and was carved from the antler of a buck. I was sitting on the grass playing with it when I heard my mother's scream. It was only then I saw the Unwanted Ones getting out of the *tapooteek*."

Kuise's thin frame convulsed with shame and guilt. With her hands covering her face, she sobbed uncontrollably. Tears ran down her smooth, brown cheeks in visible streaks.

"She was looking for me. And because I disobeyed her, she was murdered." Without looking up at her father, she braced for the blow that would come.

"Silence!" her father roared, his voice as sharp as an alder whip. Kuise cowered and shifted her hands from her face to her head to ward off her father's fury. She knew the punishment for disobedience was severe and was almost always meted out with blows to the head and back.

Kop walked toward his daughter. His countenance was fierce to look upon.

Kuise was the one thing keeping him from returning to avenge Tehonee's death. Kop had also read the sign after Tehonee's death. He had seen Tehonee's running step following Kuise's, and he knew why she went running back. He had waited for her to tell him about that day, knowing she would. Trembling with fury, he advanced toward his daughter until he stood beside her. Kuise sensed more than saw his presence and looked up. Her hands were still clasped over her small head. She looked up at her father, suddenly unafraid. Tears seeped out of her eyes as she waited for the punishment which would free her soul.

But Kop saw that the wide brown eyes and the rounded cheeks crowded with tears were Tehonee's. Kuise stared up at her father, her face drawn with grief and guilt. She waited, unafraid now, without blinking.

Then, with an indrawn breath, Kop fell down on his knees beside his daughter, and in a rare display of his love, he embraced the only remaining trace of his beloved Tehonee. It was then, while holding his daughter close, he saw that she had mended the holes in her clothes. The stitching was as though it had been done by Tehonee's own hand.

THEY MOVED THEIR camp twice more in as many evenings, expecting the whites to come searching. The sail he had stolen made building a camp easy, providing a leak-proof cover. Each night he watched the whites, and though they worked with furtive glances cast into the forest, and kept muskets close at hand, they did not pursue him into the woods. For the first three nights they kept fires blazing at the wharf end, where they had retied their boat. Kop was tempted to further harass them but decided not to. Nothing but the head of the man with the red hair would satiate him. The man was crippled by the arrow shot from Kop's bow, but he received no sympathy from the others. He was still expected to work. He did so slowly and in obvious pain and appeared to be nervous when the others were not around. He was clearly afraid of the forest. An opportunity to attack him at night was unlikely. Kop would have to attack in the daylight.

There was only one place the redhead was ever alone for a short time every day. It was when he left the others and went just beyond the edge of the woods to move his bowels. He did so around the same time each day, without fail, just before dusk, taking his musket with him. It was as if the man decided to go at dusk to avoid going out alone in the dark. Kop also noticed that it always took him a long time to relieve himself. None of the others seemed to miss him.

Kop watched from a distance. He could have shot an arrow into his throat, but he wanted to be close enough to look into the man's eyes as he died. The redhead's daily routine was his weakness. Kop knew how and where he would avenge Tehonee's death. And that same evening, the sky told him when he would do it.

SCUDDING DARK CLOUDS came up over the lip of the sea from the north. For a time the smaller islands in the distance loomed large above the sea. The air was suddenly dense, still, and sharp with cold. The first of the autumn storms was close. Rain pelt-ed the roof of his camp the next morning. Before he left, Kop told Kuise she could have a bigger fire. No one would see any smoke this day. Kop also knew the storm was only flexing its muscles for what was to come. Wrapped in a robe of deer hide that reached below his knees, Kop stepped out into the pouring rain and left camp. His head was bare. Trees leaned and bent as he brushed past.

Nothing moved outside the grey tilts. The trees swayed and the wind howled. Smoke rising from the hovels' smoke holes was sucked away by the wind. Waves rolled endlessly onto the landwash and rattled back to sea.

Huddled among the sodden trees, the Beothuk waited, ignoring the raging elements around him. Kop knew it was time for the redhead to appear. And when he did not show himself, Kop thought the man had exited the tilt to "use" sometime before the storm and he had missed him. Still, he waited. Then the door of the tilt opened, and his nemesis appeared in the doorway. The wind slammed the door shut behind him. Kop didn't hear the door close above the roaring wind. The man's head was covered against the storm. With a musket in his left hand, he advanced toward the treeline where the Beothuk waited.

Tangles of dark red hair, plastered with rain, dangled outside the man's head covering and reached all the way to his thick, short neck. His face was drawn against the storm and his mouth gaped open, showing a mouthful of blackened teeth. He was terrified of the woods, and it showed. He glanced all around and saw nothing. His breathing came in gasps, and he was shaking in fear. But Kop was not afraid. His time of revenge was at hand.

The redhead unbuttoned and dropped his pants with his right hand. He crouched down, still holding the musket in his left. His ass showed white in the shadows. With disgust, Kop noticed the man's ass was covered in red sores like his face. He looked away.

The man was suffering. He used the long gun in his left hand for purchase as well as for balance, pulling on it until it shook. His stomach muscles contracted, but his bowels were not ready. He groaned, seeking relief. It was the last sound he would ever make.

A hand clutched his chin, and with a vicious pull, his head was snapped back. Long, brown fingers, strong as stone, pinched his nostrils shut and closed his airways. Another hand closed over the fingers of the hand holding the gun. It broke two of the redhead's fingers, and the gun fell to the ground. Unable to open his mouth and desperately struggling for air, the man stared up in terror at the face looking down at him. Though he had never seen the Beothuk man whose woman he had killed and whose daughter he had tried to kill, he must have known it was him. Paralyzed beyond fear, he felt a sudden pressure, cold and sharp, against his throat.

"For my *woasut!*" Kop hissed against the man's ear. "And for Kuise!" He drew his knife against the man's throat. It was then the redhead's bowels released, and Kop let the man fall backwards into his own waste.

It had all taken but a few moments. Satisfied with his work, Kop stood. The evening had closed in. The land was grey with rain and shrouded in dense fog. Kop peered out from the copse, unmindful of the storm. No alarm had come from the tilts. Spears of light stabbed through cracks in the tilt seams. The doors did not open, and no night fire was kept burning outside. Brazenly, Kop skirted the outside edge of the camp-site until he was below the wharf. He sprang up and listened. There were only the storm sounds, louder here with the hiss of water and the crash of waves upon the shore. The boat was loaded deep in the water and stank of too many salted fish. It chafed at its moorings, tied with two lines, fore and aft. Kop cut both of them. The wind was blowing hard in the cove, and waves slapped at the vessel's sides. Her lines severed, she was quickly swept away, carried by wind and wave, and made for the jagged rocks farther in the cove. The noise of her foundering could be mistaken for wave action. No one was listening.

Back above the beach, Kop entered the woods near the redhead's body. Before long, the butt of the white man's musket was driven into the ground, and impaled upon its bayonet was the man's head. His eyes were wide open and facing the forest he feared. And without looking back, Kop disappeared into the forest.

The storm raged all night and part of the next day. It finally spent itself in the time of deep sleep on the second night, and when the dawn broke, Kop and Kuise left for the long river valley which would lead them to their winter house. The air cooled in the wake of the hurricane and leaves changed their colour and came fluttering down. The days seemed fleeting, and the nights were long and cold. For Kop and Kuise, it was now a valley of despair. This past season on the coast had not only changed their lives forever—their way of life, since before ancient memory, and foretold by the Mages, was in jeopardy. Kop saw the signs of his people on the point of every wooded bend and in the bottom of every cove on the riverbanks. But it was a dead spoor, bereft of all life, as cold as the ring of ash from once-welcome campfires he found beneath the burnt-out frames of *mamateeks*. It was as if his people had vanished forever from this valley.

14

KOPITUK HAD BEEN born where the wide river exited the Great Red Pond, halfway out a long spit of land with scattered trees, on a day when it rained hard. His mother brought him from the woods, where she had birthed him alone, and entered the comfort of a *mamateek*. Her *pushaman*, man-child, was naked and screaming. His cries went unnoticed. His mother splashed him with cold water and with her soft hands cleansed him of her birth smell. The boy cried louder.

His indignities were not over. On bended knees, his mother offered the child in her arms to his father, who stood tall above her, waiting. The father smeared red ochre on him, from his hair to his toes. Then he handed the child, who was shivering, crying, and the colour of blood, back to his mother before he left the *mamateek*. It was taboo for the father to witness a child's first drink of life. His mother bared the fullness of her breasts and guided her son to her swollen breasts. His mouth filled with its first warm nutrition, and with the comforting beat of a gentle heart against his own, the boy ceased his frantic cry and drank.

The damp nights and the dry days of autumn came. One day the boy was seated on the beach at the water's edge, clad only in a deerskin breechcloth. His mother was cleaning silvery *ouananiche* by his side. Behind her, a drying rack above a smoky fire awaited the fish. Waves washed upon the beach and over the boy's feet. The waves carried the stem of a dead plant, which had been dislodged from the lake's bottom, and it stopped between his feet. The boy, who as yet had no name, reached for it. The stalk was as thick as his wrist and as long as his arm, and he tried to drag it out of the water. His mother saw his struggles and picked up the stalk and placed it in his lap. It was what the Beothuk called *kop*, or beaver root. It still had a few sodden green leaves, and its pulpy stalk oozed a red stain. After a few minutes, the boy tired of playing with the lifeless plant.

Later that evening, when her husband returned from hunting, he brought with him two geese and one black duck. His wife showed him the beaver root and told him the water spirit had brought it to their son upon the blue waves, and he had accepted it. It was a sign for the parents, and the boy was given the name Kopituk, and as he grew older he came to be called Kop by all, except his mother, who called him by his full name.

Kopituk grew into a strong boy, swift of limb and possessing a keen eye. He swam in the shallows before he could walk. With only five seasons behind him, his arm was strong enough to draw the bow and launch the short arrows to hunt snowshoe hares. He delighted in jumping into the water and chasing fish caught in the weirs to the shallows, where they could be killed. From his father he learned these were not games but deadly skills which must be forever honed in order to provide and live. They led a nomadic way of life and, with the changing seasons, followed the animals to plain and lair, river and sea. They were hunter-gatherers. Kop learned, and before he had seen eight winters, he had killed his first doe. As he grew, he developed another trait. He often disappeared into the woods and sometimes did not return for days. Finally, when he did return, he always brought game to share. Kop was not only a fearless hunter; he was becoming a loner. His family grew to expect this and seldom searched for him, but one time Kop went missing for an entire winter. His people searched for days without success. When Kop came back to the Red Pond village early the next spring, it was empty, and Kop, the loner, went back into the valleys.

HE WALKED INTO a small camp of Beothuk, carrying a seal upon his shoulder. He had killed it with a single arrow as it lay in the sun upon the rocks just two coves over. After their initial surprise at the tall young man—who was obviously one of their kind—and seeing he had brought food, they accepted him into their camp. Some of them knew who he was and had seen him before. A tall man who appeared to be their elder approached Kop.

"You are the one who spends much time alone and who was missing from the warm lodge of your *ewinon* for all of that season of cold. Your *ewinon* looked for you long after the others had stayed in their *mamateeks*. It was the coldest of winters, and he was sad when they gave up the search. They looked for you for two more seasons."

"Where are they?" asked Kop, looking all around. The seal on his back dripped blood on his shoulders when he moved.

"They are all *winum*. We found them just upstream from the mouth of the great river near the weir."

Kop hung his head. "How did they die?"

"From the fire sticks which shoot unseen arrows, carried by the Unwanted Ones," he was told. "Their *meotick* was burned to the ground. Their fish racks stripped. No furs were found. The pointed fur *kaniskwe'te* from your mother's head was stolen."

"Even the *mu'ksans* on her feet were taken," said a short woman who had come up behind her husband. "With my own eyes I saw her sew them while she offered soft *se'kos* to the spirits for your safe return. She stained them with the red ochre and her tears."

"We buried them well above the tide waters. We put all of their possessions in the graves. There wasn't much," said her husband. The others gathered around, listening.

"There was a fight," Kop said. It was more a statement, not a question. His father would not die without fighting. This he knew.

"There was much blood on the sand at the river's edge, near the marks left by the heavy boats of the Unwanted Ones. They were bleeding when they left," the tall man answered. "And there was evidence of fighting on shore. Why do they attack and kill us without reason?"

The seal was growing heavy on his shoulders, and Kop lowered it to the ground. He noticed the others looking longingly at the fresh meat. They all looked hungry.

"In the heads of the Unwanted Ones, I believe there was a reason," said Kop. He straightened his body. He carried the limp carcass of the heavy seal far. He was looking around the campsite as he spoke. He saw a piece of sail spread on the ground, strands of rope hanging from a tree, and in the fire, rusty pieces of iron were being heated.

"I believe they came for their belongings," Kop said, pointing at the items.

"They are not their belongings! They are ours! We are not thieves. The Unwanted Ones went away before the time of cold. They left many things behind on our land. If they wanted them, why did they leave them without guarding them? No one leaves tools behind."

"They do not think as True People, who keep their belongings with them always," said Kop. "For us, items left unattended are considered discarded ones, and to take them is not a crime. We must keep hidden the strange things we find at the white men's camp." He stepped closer to the fire and turned his back to its warmth. He was soaked with blood from the seal and sweat from his shoulders. Steam drifted from his body.

He changed the subject. "There were others who shared camp with my father. Where are they?"

"We have not seen them. Though we believe they might have escaped."

Kop stood silently by the cooking fire. With his two hands cupped, he offered the Beothuk the gutted seal. It was gratefully accepted. They waited, expecting him to tell them where he had been, but he didn't speak. He would never tell them he had been careless and that when his guard was down he had heard too late the steps behind him. He had been kidnapped and held captive all winter.

WHEN SPRING RAIN and fog came, he escaped from his captors. It had been easy. After his escape and finding his village deserted, he became bitter. Instead of heading toward the sea, where he knew they had gone, he went deeper into the forest. After a long time alone in the secret valleys, he was awakened in the dark one night with a sudden urge to be among others of his kind. With the rising sun full on his face, he had left his camp to look for them. Now he had found them. He offered no explanation for his long absence, and none was asked. Kop was given a hearty welcome into their camp. He was a hunter who had brought meat.

The young girl who was ordered by her father to prepare the seal meat for cooking was called Tehonee. She approached him shyly. Her dark eyes looked up at him. He had never seen anything so lovely in his life. When he handed her the first cut of meat, their hands met, and he was in love.

When Tehonee's clan went inland to their winter house on the shores of the Great Red Pond, Kop went with them, and before the snows came, Tehonee and he had pledged their troth. They moved into their own shelter, and when the spring came, Kop led his mate away from the others and the lake of his birth. So much was Tehonee in love with Kop, she went with him willingly. Though he had taken a mate, Kop was still a loner.

They moved west and south, hunting, fishing, and gathering as they went. They crossed many tributaries which ran into the mother of rivers. On they travelled all that spring and summer until they reached the coast. They were alone and saw no others. The days of gathering food and nights of loving went quickly. The nights cooled, the geese began their flight south, and following the spawning salmon run, Tehonee and Kop headed inland again, and in the glorious autumn, Kop found what he was looking for. He had spent time here in this same valley before, all alone, and now he would share it with the woman he loved. It was a secluded valley through which a swiftly flowing river ran. The river was joined by many tumbling streams and wended its way for many miles, until it entered the ocean at the head of a long, narrow bay with many coves, beaches, and small islets covered with grass where birds nested. This valley of plenty was where Kopituk and Tehonee decided to start their new life together. Far inland, at the head of the valley, they built their first *mamateek* together by the side of a large pond where a river entered.

They who were born separate and who had pledged their

union with the bond of love and heart were now as one. They revelled in love and youth and discovery. The spring in their young muscles carried them through valleys where streams teemed with fish, and up over pine-clad ridges to brushy plains where deer wandered. The trees lost their summer green and overnight were burnished with autumn. And when the first snow came stealing down in the black of night, Tehonee had already missed her first menses. She waited till one more bleeding time had gone before she told Kop she was with child.

The winter was not a severe one, and until her belly was too heavy for safe travel, Tehonee tended the trapline with Kop. They had killed three *kosweet,* which saw them through with enough meat to stave off hunger, and soft hides to keep them warm. And when the last snow had disappeared from the south-facing hills, on a dark night sultry with spring, Tehonee went alone into their *mamateek* and tied the flap tight. Kop walked away into the trees. Tehonee was fortunate to be allowed such comfort during her time of birthing. Both hers and Kop's places of birth had been much different.

WHEN THE NIGHT had come up over the hills and the camp was drowsy, Tehonee's mother's pains began. She uttered no sound. Quietly, she walked away from the low fire where she had huddled for warmth. The night was cold and growing colder. A rising sliver of moon filtered a wan glow down through the trees surrounding the campsite. Some shadows were softened, and some were deepened with the night light. Tehonee's mother walked into them. There were others crouched by the fire who watched her leave. No one spoke to her. They knew where she was going and why she was going there. The place where she was headed had already been predetermined by her. No one would come near her chosen place of birthing. Not even if she screamed for help. It was a woman's pain to bear alone. If all went well, she would return before dawn carrying her new child.

If she died giving birth, it meant the site she had chosen was not blessed by her birth spirit. When after a night and a day she had not returned, the eldest woman of the tribe and a young girl whose first time of bleeding had not yet come followed her trail. Finding the woman perished and the newborn still living, the young girl carried the child back to camp, where it would be cared for by the women. The dead mother was buried by the elder woman at the place of her death, without ceremony. The woman who buried her would never reveal where; it was a bad omen for a woman to be taken by her death spirit at the time of her life-giving. The child would be given its name by the elders and raised a full member of the tribe. The dead mother's name would not be spoken again.

WHEN KOP THOUGHT he had gone far enough into the darkness, he stopped. When the first cry came, he knew he had not walked far enough. He shivered, transfixed by the sounds. The cries of his woman were made all the more heart-rending by the cloak of night. When Tehonee cried out, all the night sounds seemed to cease and pay heed to the ageless harbinger of new life. Kop was unable to move away from the cries or go to them. He waited. And Tehonee, who was learning hard her first painful experience of one of life's greatest mysterious, bore the pain alone. After a while, when her pains had suddenly quelled, Kop walked back to the shelter. He untied the flap and entered. Tehonee's face was damp with perspiration. Her long, black hair was plastered to her head. She looked up from her bed of fur, and her eyes shone with a new mother's wonderment. Kop had never seen her more beautiful. She washed the *imamus*, the woman-child, and swaddled her in the luxurious auburn fur of a pine marten. Then she drew the child to her breast—the left one, the one nearest to the heart.

Kop slept apart from Tehonee that night, as was fitting. Tehonee rested all that night and late the next day. She emerged from the lodge that evening and brought the child in her arms into its first light of day. Kop was adding wood to the campfire.

"Look in the sky, Kopituk!" Tehonee cried with excitement. She was looking west, where the sun was setting, and then to the east, where a huge full moon was rising. Kop drew near and stood by her side, looking into the heavens.

"It is the best of omens!" he exclaimed. "Even as the *kuis* dies in the west, the *kuise* rises in the east. The Great Spirit has blessed our *emamooset*. She will have light by day and night."

"We can call her Kuisduit?" asked Tehonee.

"It is a good name, which means the light for day and night. I will call her Kuise, for the light which sheds the night."

"Yes, my hunter."

The sun settled low until all but its hues of purple and taints of red were left trapped among the trees. The full moon rose, and when it had cleared the earth, it stopped and shone its brilliance down. Kop was standing and Tehonee was seated by the soft fire light. Kop held his daughter for the first time. She was naked but made no sound. He pointed the child toward the dying sun, then to the rising moon. Then, with great tenderness, he anointed her tiny body with the sacred red clay. The child cried then. He finished ochring the child, then placed her into Tehonee's waiting arms. She cradled the child, and she grew quiet.

"Kuisduit," Tehonee said softly, holding the girl against her chest.

"Kuise," Kop said evenly.

"Yes, my hunter." Tehonee stood with her child and entered the shelter. The wail of a male loon, boasting its spring arrival, sounded sweet and clear over the pond water. It was followed by the crooning of the mate he had chosen for life. Kop went to join his own mate, whom he had also chosen for life.

15

STANDING WITH KUISE, hidden by the trees and looking out on the water, Kop's mind was overtaken by his memories. They were beside the big lake just below the point where he had been born. Kop was torn inside. His reminiscing had brought the events of his life flooding back. It seemed as if it had all happened just yesterday, so vivid were his memories, most of them sad.

Nothing moved on the water, no stir of life on the point. He had approached the point downwind. The wind blew cool and easy toward him. There were no smells from cooking fires, no tang of woodsmoke in the air. Sitting atop the tallest tree, out the low point, were two ravens, their heads down. They clucked and croaked and preened. Kop scanned the woods and the shoreline again. Deep in the shadows created by the point and just out from the water's edge, a black duck hen was standing on one leg on a low rock. Swimming around the rock and frequently dipping their heads below the water were six of her fledglings. Their new tail feathers and pale legs bobbed above the water as their heads went below. The wary hen was as contented as the ravens. The birds felt safe. Kop stepped out on the beach, and Kuise followed him. The hen was instantly alarmed. Squawking loudly, she dashed into the water and swam away from the shore. Her young staggered after her and battered awkwardly over the calm surface before finally gaining stuttered flight. The hen shot out of the water and followed them, flying low over the water.

The ravens ceased their croaking and occasionally cawed as Kop and Kuise walked up the beach toward the long point. At the bottom of the cove where the point began, a clear brook divided the beach and ran into the lake. Father and daughter walked through its cool, shallow water and stood upon the grass on the point side of the cove. The grass and brush were well trodden by many feet. A well-worn path wound from the point to the brook where water had been gathered for drinking. Kop stopped and looked around. He had drunk from this stream many times. His people always drank from running streams, preferring the cool water to the warm lake water, which they used for cooking. Following the path he knew so well, Kop led Kuise to the edge of the trees at the base of the point.

He stopped and looked all around. He could detect nothing unusual. A small flock of honking geese in vee formation was winging its way toward the mouth of the river. The ravens on the tree were eyeing them. There were two *mamateeks* on the point. Their doorways all faced south, as was the Beothuk way. And among the trees inside the point, there was only one where there had been many. The lodges were decrepit and in disrepair. In many places birchbark hung from them and flapped in the breeze, proving there was no one in them. Motioning for Kuise to halt, Kop walked up to one of the shelters. Despite the birds showing no alarm, Kop couldn't be sure if the Unwanted Ones were inside the lodges, waiting to attack.

He approached the back of the first lodges from the north side. He held a spear in one hand and a bow in the other. Clenched in his teeth was a long arrow. Kop had come here prepared to fight. Within easy reach of the shelter, he crouched low to the ground and listened for any sounds coming from inside. The trees rustled. The waves lapped upon the shore, and the ravens croaked. There came no other sound. Still bent low to the ground, Kop walked to the door opening. The hide flap was missing, and after his eyes adjusted to the dark inside, he entered. There was nothing inside to indicate recent occupancy. There were no sleeping robes. The fir boughs on the sleeping ledges had turned brown and stiff. Mice had moved in.

Kop caught a blur of movement inside. He whirled around and in one fluid motion plucked the arrow from his mouth, placing it against his bowstring. Perched on one of the drying poles which straddled the *mamateek*, a small owl stared down at him with big eyes. Kop lowered his bow and stepped outside again. He walked out on the point, and the ravens flew away as he approached the next shelter. Not until he had searched all of the *mamateeks* out on the point did he call to Kuise, who came running to see what her father had discovered. There was nothing to show her but the footprints of the Unwanted Ones. Everything of any use was gone. No doorway flap covering remained. The Beothuk never carried their door flaps with them when they moved. Nor did they carry the heavy sleeping robes away from their winter house. Kop and Kuise walked back over the point along the beach, where he had once played and where he had learned to swim. A straight, shallow depression was there. He knew it for what it was: the keel mark of the Unwanted Ones' boat. It merely confirmed what he suspected. The Beothuk had been driven away from their beloved lake, and everything in their camp had been looted.

KOP AND KUISE reached the end of the cove and crossed the shallow brook again. Cold was seeping through the trees. Dark shadows stretched far out into the lake. A loon cried. The lodge among the trees would make a good shelter for the night. But with one last look behind, Kop led his daughter away from what used to be. He would never sleep here again.

They journeyed west and then south, down through the valleys with the green of summer gone and over the barrens flush with autumn. At the end of one such line of barrens, they followed caribou leads that became one winding trail, scarred on the bare rocks by a thousand hooves over a thousand years. Between the trees and boulders lining the ancient caribou lead, dead trees and heavy branches had been woven until a crude but effective fence had been built. It stretched all the way down to the high cliff above a river. For generations the Beothuk had used these fences as a means to corral and slaughter caribou.

Kop remembered the place well. He had taken part in the hunt. After the deer herd had entered the mouth of the fence, the Beothuk had sprung into action behind them. Youths, both male and female, yelled and threw stones at the frightened deer, which went racing into the trap. Women stood behind the fences to fortify their weak spots and screamed and waved cloth at the caribou as they galloped into the corral, where the archers and spearmen waited.

Now the fences had been broken in many places until they would no longer be effective. Someone had taken great effort to tear apart the carefully constructed fence materials. Kop saw signs where the deer were already using the gaps in the fences. The Unwanted Ones were becoming bolder, and they were moving into the interior, using Mi'kmaq as guides. Not only were the Beothuk deprived of their freedom and major food source on the coast of their island, they were now being pursued into the very heart of their homeland. The scenes he had witnessed by the ocean, and now the wanton destruction of the caribou fences, meant one thing: the Unwanted Ones were trying to starve them out of existence.

Father and daughter walked down the ridge trace. The waving birches gave off a hissing sound in the cool breeze. The fading ferns brushed their clothing as they passed. The sun was still many hands high, and the day breeze was still strong. Through the trees, they could determine glimpses of blue water flecked with white. They were nearing the pond where Kop and Tehonee had lived and loved and where Kuise had grown.

Standing still among the trees, they stared out at the campsite for a long time. Kop could see nothing amiss. There was no indication anyone had been here since he and his family had moved. Seeing her father was about to walk toward their *mamateek,* Kuise tugged on his arm and pointed to a tall white birch tree nearby.

"See here, my *ewinon,* where my mother and I drained the clear sap in springtime."

Kop turned and saw Kuise was sobbing quietly. Her small hand was covering a hole carved through the inner bark and into the white wood. Kop looked around, remembering. There were other birch trees with similar holes in them. The Beothuk cut holes in the trees and caught the sap which ran out of them in the first days of spring. It was one of the joys which showed the long winter was over. The tree sap which poured out through the holes was as clear as the purest spring water. It had a faint woodsy taste, and after drinking, it gave a burst of energy.

"Her spirit is all around. I will miss her more here, my *ewinon.*" Kuise's voice was trembling with emotion.

Kop looked at his grieving daughter and said nothing. He walked toward the lodge he and Tehonee had built. Looking inside, he saw a used sleeping robe, a basket made from birchbark, and some woven string, all that was left of Tehonee's handiwork. His sigh was loud in the empty shelter.

Kuise stayed among the trees until her father motioned to her it was safe to approach. She approached the open door timidly, not wanting to feel the emptiness of a home without a mother. She stood in the doorway beside her father until her eyes adjusted to the gloom. Then, with a sudden rush, she dived into the home and collapsed on the bedding of dried boughs where Tehonee had once slept. She buried her head in the caribou sleeping robe that had been left behind. It had patches on it, mended by her mother. There were new holes in the robe where field mice had chewed the hide and gathered some of its long hair for their nests. Kuise thrust her arms into the boughs.

Holding a hem of the blanket, she said in an astonished voice, "I can smell her scent!" She turned toward the doorway, to address her father, but only the distant trees loomed in the opening.

Kop was not at ease here. The memory of Tehonee was everywhere. He saw her coming from the tree shadows, her lithe form slipping through the trees, her arms filled with birchbark for basket weaving. She was shrouded in the wisp of smoke rising from their campfire. Her laughter was in the water as it tumbled down the rocky brook. Her voice, soft and gentle, was in the evening breeze which mourned the loss of day.

And in the stillness of the night lodge, he longed for the passion they had shared.

16

KOP WOULD HAVE preferred to build another, smaller *mama-teek* somewhere else, but the season was late. Already during the night, the cove was covered over with ice, and though by midday the sun had melted it, the season of cold was upon him. It was too late to start another camp. There was another, more urgent worry. The deer had not come down from their summer barrens to winter on the edge of the big timber. The deer had always come. Some years they came in great numbers, and some years they were fewer. But for some reason, this year their numbers were drastically lower. Even the winds had become contrary, and the migrating birds had rafted far out on the lake and seldom came to shore.

He hunted farther afield and often brought only scant game back to their camp. More and more often his traps were empty, and Kop knew why. Almost everywhere he went he found evidence of the Unwanted Ones. At times he hid like a shadow as they lumbered past him. And almost always leading the trappers was the ever watchful Mi'kmaq. Kop found their traps of steel and threw them in the water or stamped them down bog holes, far from where they had been set. And when he found animals in the steel traps, he carried them back to his camp.

Kuise foraged for berries and the roots of plants and gathered firewood. She mended garments as her mother had taught her, and soon her stitching resembled Tehonee's. She cooked food, mostly for herself, for each time her father returned from the hunt he was even more bitter and had resorted to eating most of his food raw. He was becoming as lean as the wolf and just as wary. It was the driest season Kop had ever seen. Without the rains to cool them, the rivers were showing their rocky beds. Brooks and streams dried up. Minnows were trapped in stagnant pools, where they died and rotted. Birds and foxes feasted on them, and when he found them, Kop ate the ones still alive. Here at the end of the pond, far from the sea, salmon had beaten their way inland and found the beds of their birth dry—as dry as the waiting weirs. The salmon schooled at the river mouth in deeper water, where they jumped and splashed and finned the water day and night. Black bears jumped after them in deep water, without much success.

The few salmon Kop and Kuise managed to catch were black and as slinky as eels. Their flesh were without fat, and their bellies were slack and empty. Kop devoured the rich, pink spawn of the females. But Kuise, who could not stomach the slimy salmon eggs, ate only their smoked flesh. Hung to dry on the smoke rack, the salmon, exhausted from their journey upstream, did not give off the rich aroma they should have.

The nights were cold and dry. Eels making their annual run to the faraway sea writhed over the dry river bottom or slithered through the damp night grasses toward deeper water. Kop, who knew their ways, sometimes waited in the dark and caught them. But it still wasn't enough. Snow clouds made the short days dark. Leaves, still green, bent and drooped and wilted under the weight of snow.

Even the hares were not prepared for the snow. They hid in balled bunches, thinking they were camouflaged. Kop shot the few he saw, their summer-brown bodies stark against the white snow. Snowshoe hare populations came in seasons of plenty, always followed by seasons of scarcity. For a season or two they peaked, and usually after seven seasons, their numbers dwindled. Kop had seen this happen before. He knew the seventh season had passed, and few of the tasty animals came to his snares, which he had made from the thin brown roots of spruce saplings. There were no young hares bouncing down the leads, and the few adults were alone and not paired.

Kop fashioned snow walkers to make travel in the deep snow easier. He bent green alder into bows, laced their shanks together, and filled the centres with deerhide webbing. He made one of the pairs smaller for Kuise, who said her snow walkers looked like swallowtails. Rawhide cut into thin strips were used for bindings.

Deep snow choked the trails early, and deer did not come down their forest traces like they had before. For days Kop concealed himself, waiting for them to come snorting and snuffling through the deep snow. He preferred a fat doe or a fawn or two. He knew the meat of the stags would be tainted, their strong annual sex drive sending their castor-like scent throughout their bodies. Kop and Kuise needed hides for clothing and footwear. But they desperately needed meat. He would kill whatever came down the trail. But though he waited for days and always walked parallel to them and never once stepped in the caribou leads, nothing came.

HE KEPT SEARCHING for food. The ptarmigan he found walking over the deep snow jumped into sudden flight almost under his feet and flew away low over the ground, cackling.

They seldom flew far. Seeing where they had landed, Kop crept after them. Sometimes he was lucky enough to get a brace. From the ground he shot grouse gathered high in the branches of spruce trees. Sometimes the birds fell down, and other times he had to climb up after them. Partridge and grouse were easily cleaned. Kop placed them face up, with wings spread. Then stepping on both wings and pushing his fingers through the flesh where the neck met the breast, he gave a quick pull. The plump, pink breasts came away from the carcass, free of feathers. But now every morsel of food was precious, and they ate the entire bird, including its viscera.

It was necessary for the Beothuk to hunt farther and farther afield. And as he went farther away from the pond where they were camped, he left Kuise behind. Already the young girl was the true keeper of the lodge. She removed dry boughs from their sleeping platforms and replaced them regularly with fresh ones. She cooked their scant meals. She gathered firewood and tended fire inside the lodge. And to ward off the winter wind she packed snow on the outside lower walls of their shelter. Kuise remembered when she and her mother had done this chore. Tehonee had made it a happy time. They threw snow at each other and laughed while they carried out the work.

Day after day her father returned empty-handed, always after dark. The long tramp on snow walkers and the lack of food, coupled with the despair of unsuccessful hunts, were taking their toll on the hunter. Kop was lean to the point of being gaunt. Still he hunted. He had to. They were running out of food.

One night, Kop was repairing a broken snow walker binding by the light of the fire. Kuise bent over the fire and added dry wood. It was very cold outside the lodge, and inside there was a white rime of frost from the floor to the lower half of the walls. The fire snopped and sizzled, and where the smoke spiralled upwards to the smoke hole and met the cold air, creosote was forming in shiny black smears.

Kuise had finally caught a buck hare in one of the snares she herself had set in a dense alder bed nearby. Its fur was a mottled white and brown. It wasn't fat and plump but long and lean. However, it was good food, and when her father entered the lodge, she was roasting it on a spit above the fire, with only its front paws missing. Kop made no comment about the meat spitted over the fire.

Kop was thinking his daughter was a better hunter than he. It made him all the more bitter. The hare dripped its juices onto the hot coals, and the tantalizing aroma wafted to his nostrils. Despite his feelings, he was salivating. He finished his snow walker repair and was about to place them against the lodge wall outside the door flap—he had long since learned that snow walkers left in the warmth when first exposed to the cold air quickly gathered snow—when Kuise spoke to him.

"Wait, my *ewinon.*"

His daughter rose from her place by the fire with the cooked hare, still on the spit, dangling golden brown from her hand. The hare was very hot. Handling it nimbly, Kuise grabbed the hindquarters and tore both of them away. Part of the animal's broken spine came with it. She handed the choicest piece to her father. Kop took the meat from his daughter and began eating ravenously.

Kuise lodged the remaining meat down, and without eating, she crawled to the shadowed side of the *mamateek.* When she came back under the light again, she held the two front paws of the hare in her hand and stood beside her father, who was still tearing at the flesh of the roasted hare with his strong white teeth. He looked up when his daughter spoke again.

"The spirit that walks unseen through the forest sent the hare, front feet first, into my withy snare. It was still alive and waiting for me to end its time. I replaced the bloody snare with a new one, as you showed me. In my first memory of snow, I saw you wear the front paws of a hare on your snow walkers. Then you always brought meat on your shoulder. Can I tie them to your snow walkers again?"

She showed her father the tufted paws. Kop swallowed a mouthful of meat, wiped grease from his mouth with his shirt sleeve, and was about to deny Kuise's request. But the sincere look on his daughter's face stopped him, and he suddenly remembered who had tied the front feet of a hare to his shoes. It seemed like a lifetime ago. Tehonee had added the tassels for show. They bounced with every step he took. Kuise was right about one thing: he had always brought game home when he wore them. He didn't tell Kuise who had tied them to his snow walkers. Kop never spoke Tehonee's name aloud.

"It is good to tie them to my snow walkers, Kuise. But you must make sure to tie the right paw to the right foot and the left one to the left," he said.

Kuise looked at the paws in her hand and the snow walkers on the floor. She could not see any difference in either of them. But Kop, who had made his own snow walkers, could tell them apart at a glance. He showed Kuise the difference. Then he took the two paws from her hand and spread them apart until the bony toes were splayed.

"See the small bend of the foot inwards. One to the left and one to the right."

Kuise, who was delighted to have her father show her

something, sprang to work while she still remembered how to do it. She tied the paws, one to each snow walker as directed, with a thin leather thong. When she had finished, Kop took the snow walkers and placed them outside the door. When he drew back the hide flap, a wisp of cold air sucked inside the lodge, where it met the warm air inside to create a thin, cold fog. For a moment, stars were framed in the door opening. It gave the lodge a little more light. Kop drew the flap closed, the fog dissipated, and the shelter was draped in shadow again.

WHEN KOP CAME down over the ridge the next evening, night was behind his shoulder, and upon it was the full carcass of a deer. His step was laboured and clumsy. Kuise, who was longing for her father's return, heard him coming. She squealed with delight when she saw his catch. So great was the girl's delight at seeing fresh meat draped across her father's back, she paid little mind to the way he staggered. Kop had not stopped to eat all day, and his muscles were drained of energy. He let the carcass slide from his shoulders near the *mamateek* door. The sudden relief made him stagger all the more, and he fell backwards upon the deer. He was sweating and looked done in.

Kuise ran to his side, and seeing his weariness for the first time, she ignored the bounty of meat and helped pull him to his feet. She had never seen the need to aid her father in anything before, and it startled her. She noticed the bag Kop always carried on a sling over his left shoulder was damp with blood. She took it from him and drew out what she knew would be there. The deer viscera fell from her hands onto the snow. She bent down and with her own knife cut a piece from the heart muscle. She handed it to her father, and Kop took the meat and stuffed it into his mouth. Blood ran down his chin as he chewed, and Kuise bent to cut him another piece.

That night, Kop and Kuise feasted on the deer meat. Their bellies were satiated for the first time in days, and father and daughter were in good spirits. Kop was so relaxed when Kuise asked him about the hunt, he told her how it had gone. It is the way of hunters to relive the hunt, and the telling of it, even to an audience of one, relieved much of the stress. And Kuise was the best of listeners.

"It was late, with only one hand of light left, when I saw the spoor," Kop began. "The track was deep in the snow, and though I could not yet tell if it was stag or doe, I could see the *kosweet* was struggling hard. I followed the track. The deer was keeping to the heavy trees, where the snow was not so deep. Hunger betrayed my step. My snow walkers clicked together. The sound was loud in the deep woods, and the *kosweet* heard me. I could tell by its broken stride."

Standing, Kop warmed to the story. The four haunches of meat hung above the campfire just above his eye level. Smoke drifted among them, crusting and curing them. He reached up and cut a small piece from one of the quarters, then gently wound the quarters till their hanging thongs were taut. When he released them, the deer haunches slowly turned in the smoke. Kop chewed on the meat with relish and not from hunger. The smell and the taste of the fresh venison—dark, smoky, and juicy—spurred him on, and he continued to tell Kuise of the hunt.

HE HAD REMOVED his hide coat and left his spear behind, preparing for a long hunt. It was the only track he had seen for weeks, and he fully intended to run the deer down, no matter how long it took. But the Great Spirit was with him, he told Kuise, and when the deer broke out of the woods into even deeper snow, he caught his first glimpse of it. It was a doe, and it was foundering badly in a deep snowdrift at the bottom of a deep ravine not far away. Kop experienced the hunter's flush, and for the moment, all of his recent deprivations were forgotten. The thrill of the stalk surged through his veins, and thus buoyed, he ran after the deer.

He could see plumes of steam spouting from its nostrils and jaws. It turned to see Kop running on its trail and frantically tried to break free, but its efforts only drove it deeper into the drift. There was no need for stealth now. Even with the snow walkers, his feet sunk deep. His calf muscles were burning, and he rasped for breath. He wished now he had brought his spear. The light was fading fast, and he wanted a quick kill. Twice Kop stumbled, once when a snow walker became snarled in the other, and he fell. Getting to his feet, he forced himself to take more care. The caribou had sunk to its neck in snow. It was winded and going nowhere. He suddenly realized he had never been so hasty on a hunt before. He had never been so hungry, either.

The stricken doe's eyes rolled, and the whites of them showed streaks of red. Kop drew his knife. It was one he had taken from the Unwanted Ones. His favourite. The long, straight one. He had honed it daily. He jumped astride the deer. The animal bleated piteously and tried to get its hooves above the snow, but it was no use. Kop's weight on its back prevented it from ever rising again. He grabbed the animal by its tines. Its throat skin stretched tight, and its final cry was halted by the knife drawn across its throat. Blood poured from the wound, and Kop released his grip. The doe's head fell over. Its tongue fell sideways out of its mouth. The teeth clenched upon the pink tongue, and with its eyes wide open, it let out its final breath.

When Kop returned to the deep woods again, all but the doe's entrails and its head were upon his shoulders. He would have taken the head with him, but the weight was too great. He had pointed the head in the direction the deer's spirit had wanted to go and with great difficulty had shouldered the carcass. The doe was not as fat as it should have been. Its flanks were lean, and the ribs were laddered along its sides. But it was badly needed meat. Even the fleet-footed deer were having trouble finding food. Back in the woods again, the light was all but gone.

"I followed my own tracks back. It made my way easier. But I was heavily laden and my step was slow and . . . listen!" Kop hissed. He stopped speaking.

The sudden silence was heavy in the lodge. A fire coal crackled. The haunches of caribou turned slowly.

Kuise's eyes, big and round, bore into her father's face. Kop was as still as a dry tree trunk. His arms hung in mid-air, and his face was a mask of concentration. His head was turned askance, like a fox straining to hear above a mouse hole in deep snow. There was nothing to hear. Kuise stirred. The boughs under her rustled as she did so. Kop's hand motion stopped her from questioning him. And then it came again! The long, drawn-out howl of a wolf. It was far away. But the night was still, clear, and frosty. Even in the midst of his telling, Kop had heard its first cry.

"Wolves always howl after they have found food," Kop told Kuise. "This one is a male who has found my kill. He is calling for his mate to share."

They listened intently. The lone wolf call came again. It was in the same place. And still no answering call was heard.

"I have heard their howls at night many times, my *ewinon*," Kuise said. "I have seen only one in the light of day. Still their howls at night frighten me."

"This one howls alone, Small One. Maybe he has no mate to answer him."

Kuise stared at her father, seeing the pain of his loss in his eyes. The wolf's lament came again.

"It is not the wolf that howls you must fear, Small One. It is the wolf that prowls you must be wary of."

17

THE LONG NIGHTS of winter seemed endless. But finally, the southern sun dominated. The nights grew shorter, the days were longer and warmer, and the big melt began. Geese returned to the frozen ponds. It was a time without spring. Kop and Kuise were fast running out of food again. The leg bones of the doe had been cooked over the fire, cracked open, and the rich yellow marrow inside devoured.

The snow was deep and soft, and even wearing snow walkers was not good for travel, but they had to move from their wintering valley and find food. They would travel in the early morning, when the snow was crusted from the night's frost and walking made easy.

What was left of the deer was packed during the night with their meagre belongings. They left their heavy sleeping robes in the lodge. And in the morning, when the slayer of night was only a pale glow in the east, Kop opened the hide door and led Kuise away from their winter house.

The snow pack was melting deep beneath its crusted surface. Water ran in every seam of land. Streams and brooks became torrents of icy water and had to be crossed. Winding rivers overflowing their banks straightened and became impassable barriers of rushing white water. Sea-run salmon, gaunt and hungry, were swept gloriously to sea, their journey downstream far different from the one they had made upstream. They were all but impossible to catch. In places Kop and Kuise could not get close enough to the swollen riverbanks to gather the shrivelled red squashberries. Although the fruit tasted bitter, it was still food. But now the black water engulfed the plants. It twitched and pulled at the drowned stems, causing the red berries on the branches to bend and sway, as if mocking them.

Hunger made their journey longer and harder. To add to their misery, it rained for days and days. Walking over the rotting snow demanded energy they did not have. At night they slept fitfully under dripping boughs and covered themselves with light hides and a ragged strip of ship canvas.

Kop had decided to return to the sea. It was the only place where he was sure to find food. They ate the last of their venison. Grouse they managed to kill were at their spring leanest, their flesh rangy and tough. Kop threw them in the fire, still feathered, and he and Kuise chewed right down to the small wing bones.

They dug out pallid roots of cattails and ate them in boggy leads free of snow. From the streams they managed to catch a few sticklebacks and trout minnows, which they ate raw. They drank birch sap, which had started running again. It gave them energy but contained no nutrients. They would have to find food or die of starvation.

WHEN THEY ARRIVED at the coast, the sight that met their eyes was not a good one. For as far as they could see, the ocean was an unbroken sea of ice. It had arrived early. Ice had crowded in every tickle and grounded in every cove. So wide was the great white plain that the might of the rollers at its outer edge was not felt upon its inner edge. There was no sundering of ice against the rocks, only the daily ebb and flood of the tide to jar the imprisoned ice pack. Not one open lead of water could be seen. Open water among the ice would mean birds and seals. They watched ducks come soaring in and, finding no water, fly away again and pitch down in some open lead far away from shore.

At ebb tide, father and daughter dipped their hands into the icy water and plucked snails and mussels from the rocks until their hands were numb. The shoreline up as far as the tidewater could reach was free of snow, and Kop and his daughter walked it with ease. Above the shoreline, among the tangled tress bent by the wind, the snow, greying and dirty with winter debris, was still deep and too soft to walk upon. Wherever possible, Kop and Kuise walked the landwash. Their steps were weak and staggered. Kuise's step was pitiful. Gone was her bounding spring. She leaned on a staff of driftwood she had found. She drank water at every stream they crossed. Kuise had developed the act of constantly swallowing, and her belly was swelling.

It was the sound of gunfire—not the tantalizing aroma of roasting meat—which drew them, slightly above the gravelly cove, beside a brook where the Unwanted Ones were hunched over a bright campfire. There were two men above the fire, upon which the full carcass of an otter was roasting. One of them was examining the otter pelt, which was springtime ragged and lacked its usual lustre. The other was tending to the fire and the meat. There were two guns at the ready near them. The smell of the meat wafted to the two Beothuk, and Kop's craving for food nearly betrayed him. He held himself in hiding and motioned for Kuise to take cover with him. He looked at his daughter. Her face was thin and haggard. Her leggings were ripped, her tunic was torn, and one of her moccasins revealed bleeding toes. Looking at his young daughter now, Kop seemed to realize for the first time how dire their situation was. The glint had gone from her eyes. She was trembling head to toe. Kop had never heard Kuise complain about anything, and now she was silently starving to death.

Kop, too, was weak from hunger. They were both wet and cold. But he was sweating now, after he made a decision. Both father and daughter were crouched on snow among the trees. The two men on the beach had no idea they were being watched.

The one tending the fire plucked a piece from the otter's hot flesh. The meat was hot and sticky, not yet cooked, and the man handled it quickly between his fingers before pushing it between his bearded lips. The other man growled at him.

Kuise, who was now seated on the snow and too weak to stand, tapped her father's knee and pointed to the snow around them. Kop tore his eyes from the scene below and saw several tiny grey moths emerging from the snow. His face relaxed and his fierce eyes softened at seeing his daughter's face, in the time of her deepest despair, yet still cognizant of her world. Her simple gesture only reinforced Kop's decision. The moths stumbled on the snow, straining for their first flight. One of them rose into the air.

Sunlight poured through the trees. The time of warmth and plenty was coming, but it would not arrive fast enough to help Kuise. Kop stood and helped her up. He picked up his long spear in one hand, his bow and quiver of arrows in the other, and with his spear hand on the handle of the knife at his side, he stepped into full view of the Unwanted Ones. And at his stern command, Kuise followed him.

For several heartbeats the men on the beach didn't notice the silent Beothuk in their midst. Then they saw them. The one crouched near the fire scrambled sideways like a crab for his gun. In his haste he knocked the otter carcass into the smouldering ashes. The other stood up tall, his gun already in hand.

It was then Kop dropped first his spear and then his bow and arrows. They clattered on the beach as they fell. He pulled the knife of steel from its sheath and let that drop, too. The blade clinked on the stones. Kuise stood by her father's side, shivering in fear, and they stepped away from the weapons.

The strangers' guns were the same weapons which Kuise had witnessed spilling fiery death into her mother's breast. It seemed like just yesterday. Her legs grew weak, and she grabbed her father's hand for support. Kop took her cold and trembling hand in his, and raising his left hand to his head, he stepped forward. It was then Kop realized he wasn't holding a green bough—the sign of peace—as he had intended. But surely he would not need a peace bough, now that they could plainly see he was unarmed. He dropped his left arm to his side, his hand open, palm outward and empty.

The two Unwanted Ones had crossed the river mouth, which was kept free from sea ice by its spring torrent, just after dawn that morning. They had walked south on the landwash searching for whatever they could find. The sea all around them was choked with ice. They could neither fish nor hunt on the sea. Their larders were nearly bare. They had spotted the otter fishing in the river mouth. It had climbed out on a rock near the shore and was chewing on its catch when they killed it.

Now they were startled by what stood before them. Two Beothuk Indians, with long, matted black hair, dressed in tattered hides. One was smaller than the other. Still, they were Indian. They watched the taller one drop his weapons on the beach and step away from them. They heard the rattle of the weapons falling and saw that his hands were empty. Then the tall one, speaking loudly in his savage tongue, stepped toward them. The smaller of the two was shouting in the same guttural language, and now both extended hands cupped like beggars.

It went against Kop's very soul to stand without weapons before the Unwanted Ones. He had good reason to hate them all. Without his hunting tools, he felt naked. When he dropped his hand to his side, he stopped walking toward the two hunters. Kuise, still holding her father's right hand, stopped beside him. Kop squeezed her hand and spoke in a voice that was loud and clear, as was fitting when a hunter entered another's camp.

"I am hunter without food. Small One is a young *be'nam*, and her belly is long empty. Though my woman is *winum* by your hands, I come in peace. It is the way of all hunters to share *aschautch*. You have killed a young *edru*. Its hide is worthless, but its flesh is fat and tender."

The two astonished white men stood with guns pointed at the Beothuk. They had heard terrible tales of the Beothuk, of attacks followed by beheadings and constant thievery. Neither of them had actually seen a Beothuk before, but they were terrified of them. Now two of the Indians were standing before them, yelling in the unintelligible language of the savages, first the tall one and now the other.

When Kop finished talking, he motioned to Kuise to speak as he had instructed her.

"I am Kuise, girl child of Kopituk the great hunter. It is right for a hunter, weak from the chase, to be offered the first meat cut."

Kuise fought to control her voice. Kop had told her that to show fear to the Unwanted Ones would be a sign of weakness. She held both hands cupped together, her small palms trembling. It was the universal sign of someone asking for food. Kuise was about to speak again when the guns exploded like thunder. Her legs crumpled under her, and without a sound she slumped to the ground. Her small frame twitched once, then once again, and was still.

Kop could not believe what was happening. He had come in peace, seeking food, but had been served death. Instinctively, he whipped around, quick as a cat, and lunged for his weapons. He had almost reached them, his fingers closing on his spear, when something stabbed him in the shoulder like a hot, blunt spear point. The impact spun him around, and he saw smoke rising from the long guns. A sickening wave of nausea overtook him. His skin felt clammy. He felt faint and was going down. Through eyes glazed with pain, his head dizzy, Kop saw Kuise lying on the beach, unmoving. He was surprised to see red ochre oozing from her small chest.

THE CRY OF a seagull woke Kop from unconsciousness. The sun was warm on his face. His first thought was, *The time of warmth has come at last.* He had to force his eyes open. Kuise was lying next to him. A lone seagull was pecking at her toes through the hole in her moccasin. Then Kop moved. A cry of pain escaped him. The seagull flew away, and Kop vomited a thin bile out of his mouth and fainted. When he opened his eyes again, the gull was back. Kop pushed himself to his elbows. The gull ran down to the slope of the beach, jumped into the air, and landed on one of the clumpers of ice which crowded the cove. Reaching for Kuise, pain surged through his shoulder. It brought the nausea back, and he fought the fainting sensation. This time he stayed awake. Blood was crusted high on his right shoulder and had soaked through his shirt. His right ear felt jagged, sticky. Wincing in pain, he raised his hand to it. The lobe of his ear was missing, and his hand came away bloody.

Kop half rolled, half pushed his body until he was leaning over his daughter. He cradled her small body to his own. Tears welled in his eyes. Kuise had died with the same small hole in the centre of her chest as had her mother. There was a much bigger hole in the child's back where the ball had exited. Her blood was cold on his fingers. Sick with physical pain and mental torment, the Beothuk felt a primordial wail of misery erupt from his throat. It rolled upwards and over the treetops. It resounded across the cove and out over the great white plain, and its echo went on and on. The seagull flew away and did not return.

Dusk came, and Kop was on his feet, dazed with pain. His right shoulder burned but bled only when he tried to move his arm. His ear was numb but wasn't bleeding anymore. His body was burning up, and he craved water. Tearing himself away from his dead daughter, he staggered to the brook running out of a budding aspen copse at the end of the cove. Lying prone, he drank till he was full. Beneath a bank in the brook, thick black mud dripping with meltwater caught his eye. Crawling to it, he drew the laces from his tunic and saw the extent of his shoulder wound. Twisting his neck to better see the wound caused him more pain. Cupping water in his hand from the brook, he splashed it over the wound again and again. The cold water gave him some relief, and the cleansing showed the laceration to be smaller than it had first appeared. Kop's reflexes, the slope of the beach, and the white men's hurry had saved him. The shot had fired up the beach, intended for the centre of his chest, when he turned suddenly, and it had pierced his earlobe, entered his right shoulder, glanced upwards off the bone, and exited his body, leaving a thin red furrow at the very top of his neck. The shocking blow to his shoulder bone had knocked him out, and the two hunters had thought he was dead.

He squeezed most of the moisture from a handful of fibrous black mud. Mixing it with the pale green leaves of gowithy, he mashed it together and packed it against the wound. Then he laced his tunic tight. Stuffing his mouth full of the leaves, he chewed them to a pulp and swallowed the juices. Feeling a measure of relief, he got to his feet and walked back to the beach. The fire was out. Even in his dazed condition, Kop could plainly see by the deep prints in the beach that his attackers had fled north.

In their haste to get away, the whites had abandoned the otter carcass. It had settled in the grey ashes, and though burnt in places, it was still good food. Kop was feverish from hunger. Crouching over the dead ashes, he pulled the otter free and brushed some of the ashes off. It was still warm, and beneath the burnt skin, the flesh was pink and succulent. Kop ate ravenously for only a short time and was surprised when his stomach felt suddenly full. He was still very weak. He dropped the carcass and staggered to his feet, turning to the more immediate task at hand.

TWO DAYS LATER, Kop had finished eating most of the otter carcass. The pelt, though of poor quality, was still of use to him, and it still had its liner of yellow fat as well as tasty pieces of meat stuck to it. The whites had skinned the animal poorly. Kop was feeling stronger in body, but his spirit had been broken. He went about the work he had to do in a careless daze. He used more mud on his wound and added the pulp of inner aspen bark and the ground-up stickiness of budding dogwood to the ingredients. Later, he cleaned the wound again. Squeezing myrrh from the bladders of fir trees, he covered his wounds with the clear glue.

His shoulder and upper arm were covered with a purplish hue and were very sore, but Kop ignored the pain.

All of his hunting tools had been stolen. His knife sheath hung empty from his waist. Kop would miss the knife most of all. He needed one now. He wanted to cover Kuise's feet in the soft otter fur. One end of the beach had a rock outcropping of slate. He soon found a piece that looked right. Using a harder stone, he had to smite the slate rock several times before he managed to cleave the pieces he was looking for. They were as sharp as his stolen knife but would not keep their sharpness the same. He placed one piece in his knife sheath, two in his pack, and with one in his hand he walked toward his daughter's body.

Kop waded across the brook in the icy water to the south-facing side with Kuise's body in his arms. He placed the last true trace of his breed in a shallow hole he had dug with sharp rocks and his hands. Kuise's feet and legs were now laced with the otter fur. From her knees up to her chin she was draped with the soft middle bark of the birch tree. He had no red clay to anoint her with. If he survived, he would return later, exhume her body, and carry out the sacred ceremony.

He gently covered her face with layers of green boughs, assuring the scent of the forest spirit would stay with her in her afterlife. He crossed the brook again and again, bringing the clean slate rocks to finish Kuise's burial mound. When he was finished, it was twilight, and an evening breeze had come from out of the dark forest. The tide was receding, and aided by the offshore wind, it was pulling the ice pack away from the beach.

Kop headed north.

18

THEY STOLE INTO his camp in the dark, just after he had closed his eyes in sleep, when a tired man sleeps the soundest. They crept up to his bed of hastily gathered boughs and poked at him with their spears without cutting him. Kop opened his eyes and stared at them. They stepped back in alarm, clearly afraid of him. They kept taunting and poking him at arm's length. Kop showed no fear, only disdain. And though they were many and he was alone, it made them all the more afraid of him. They motioned him upright and kept poking him with their spear points and pushed at him until his back was to a tree, where they tied him. Even then they kept their distance from him, as if still not trusting him. They yelled and spat at him, but Kop bore it all in silence, his eyes stabbing hatred at them. His shoulder ached and burned and had started bleeding again.

He knew who they were. Their skin without the red ochre was almost the same colour as his own. Many of them were dressed in deerskins. But some of them wore the garb of the Unwanted Ones. Still tied, he was escorted away, well guarded. Kop was weak from exhaustion, hunger, and his wounds.

He had followed the shoreline for days. He ate the salty belted kelp, which had been torn from the bottom and brought to shore by the ice floes. The ice had shifted from shore but still ranged in plain sight. Pans of ice dripping meltwater were everywhere. His diet consisted of shellfish and water. He saw no one, but at the mouth of a brook one day he saw a boat tied to shore. Tracks led into the woods. Without hesitation, Kop walked to the bow of the boat, untied the rope securing it, and pushed it off. The current from the brook carried the boat away. It bumped loudly against an ice pan, wheeled off with wind and tide, and floated out to sea.

At another brook on another day, he found a net slung across a deep pool just up from its sea mouth. Kop waded out in the cold water. He found several sea trout and one large salmon. He took all the fish and slashed at the net, which drifted only as far the nearest rocks, where the swirling tide tore it into a useless tangle. For days after, he found nothing to eat. He had wandered inland, starving again, when the Mi'kmaq found him.

After walking from darkness till dawn and prodding Kop, they entered a campsite. Kop, who had smelled the camp long before they reached it, saw the two structures built there were similar to his own summer *meoticks*. As they broke through the woods below the campground, several others rushed forward in greeting. Some of them were women, and seeing the Beothuk in their midst, one of them cried out in fear.

"Why have you brought the *osa'yani* into our camp? He will call on his evil spirits from the Great Red Pond! We have no defence against such evil!"

The hysterical woman was chastised into silence by one of Kop's captors. She cried out again and fled across the compound to one of the wigwams and stood outside the door.

A man appeared from one of the wigwams, taller than the others and wearing buckskins shiny with use. He looked sharp-eyed, and in his hand he held the long gun of the Unwanted Ones. The tall Mi'kmaq stepped forward until he was face to face to Kop. The others stopped their chatter and noise as he approached. He looked defiant and unafraid. Kop kept his eyes on the musket in the man's hand.

"Why have you brought the red man to my camp with his hands bound tight?" His voice was loud and demanding.

One of Kop's captor's spoke, a short, squat man with an air of self-importance.

"The red man was hunting in the deep valley far west of the waters which feed the Great Red Pond. He has strayed far west of his boundaries." The man was shouting needlessly, a sure sign that he was afraid of the Beothuk.

The tall one said in an even, sure voice, "This man has not strayed anywhere. He walks a sure trail, and even now, bound and alone, he shows no fear." The speaker shifted his steely eyes to Kop's ear, his blood-soaked shoulder, and his gaunt features before he continued. "He is hunter. He is also wounded."

His eyes looked around at the men who had brought Kop into his camp, as if demanding to know who had attacked the Beothuk. One of them was about to speak when Kop said in a clear voice, "They are not the ones who wounded me. It was the death sticks of the Unwanted Ones, one of which you carry in your hand."

The tall one gave Kop a startled look, and the others gasped. The captive had spoken to them in their own language! The tall one shifted on his feet and cradled the gun in the crook of his arm. No one said anything. Silence prevailed. It was broken by the woman who had been chastised, shouting across the clearing.

"He is the one! He chopped off the head of the red-bearded one! The whites are searching for him."

Without turning around, the tall one held up his hand and the woman fell silent again.

"Is it as she says?" He looked steadily into Kop's eyes.

"It is as she says," said Kop.

"You know our tongue." It was a statement, not a question.

"I was prisoner of your kind."

"You are Kopituk. The one who slept in our winter house and escaped when spring came."

"I am Kop. I was not your slave."

"You were worth two muskets to the white trappers then—dead! Now you are worth five muskets to the white chiefs—alive."

"My spirit is already dead. Will they give you two muskets or five?"

The tall Mi'kmaq seemed to be looking into Kop's very soul, so intense was his stare. Kop stared back.

"Release him!" the tall one barked.

"Release the red devil in our camp?" This from the short man, who stood well behind Kop.

"There are devils in all camps. I see no red on him. Release him!"

It was true. Kop's skin had lost its red taint. The short man behind him moved with an exaggerated step. Reaching out with his knife drawn, he was about to cut Kop's fetters when the tall one shouted at him again.

"Untie him! Is your lodge so hung with leather you can waste it by a useless cut?"

The man sheathed his knife. Extending his hand toward Kop, he untied him. Kop immediately drew his arms forward. The man behind him sprang back in alarm. Grimacing with pain, Kop flexed his arms up over his body. They had been tied behind him for hours, and his muscles were sore and tense. Those around him stood ready to fight. The tall one, who still stood unafraid in front of the Beothuk, had not moved. Now he stepped aside and said for all to hear, "There is meat for the hunter at my campfire."

KOP STAYED WITH the small band of Mi'kmaq. His association with them was tenuous. Some of them hated him. A few grew to accept him. Their Mi'kmaq chief, who told Kop he was called Jimijon by the whites, was one of the latter. They had all heard the tale of the young Beothuk who had been kidnapped by a band of Mi'kmaq and who had been kept captive for a full winter before he escaped. Kop told Jimijon he could have escaped at any time that winter so long ago. But because he was of value to them, the Mi'kmaq had taken good care of him and Kop ate well.

Kop's sharp mind had picked up their language. He was aided in this, he told Jimijon, by a young boy who was fascinated by the Beothuk in their midst. By learning the new tongue, Kop soon discovered he was to be traded for guns to the white trappers in the spring. When the days warmed and the Mi'kmaq band was making ready to leave their winter house for the coast, Kop had simply left their camp one night. He ran away over the snow crust, walked down a stream, stepped out on a rocky ledge, and disappeared in the forest without a trace.

"You were alone. Your death spirit was near when my people found you," said Jimijon.

Kop knew it was the Mi'kmaq way to get answers without asking questions. He looked all around. They were seated on the ground beside a campfire outside Jimijon's lodge. The day was warm with a light breeze sighing through the green-ing trees, where birds twittered. The Mi'kmaq had little food to spare. The winter had been a long and hard one for them, too. Game was scarce. Some of them begrudged the food and care the Beothuk was given, but under strict orders from Jimi-jon, he was nursed back to health. His shoulder wound was seen to by one of the Mi'kmaq women. She was old and wise in the way of wounds, and though she was afraid of him, she tended his wound. With food and rest, he recovered quickly. His shoulder still gave him pain with certain movements, and he would forever have a notch in his ear.

"When the death stick speaks, the death spirit listens," said Kop, his eyes fixed upon the gun which never left Jimijon's hand.

Jimijon saw the hatred for the gun in Kop's eyes. He ran his hand along the length of the smooth barrel of the flintlock, his fingers stopping on the gun's action. He motioned across the campground, where the old woman who had tended Kop's wound was rubbing a mixture of ashes and urine over a black bear hide hung from a drying rack.

"We are the Bear Clan. The dog bear ventured out of his den too soon. Its spirit knew we were hungry. No arrow could reach it. In my hands the white man's gun roared like thunder, and the bear gave his life for ours—and yours."

"My Small One, who died when the death stick spoke, loved the tender flesh of the *gwashuewet* cub," said Kop.

"Bear cub meat is good." Jimijon nodded his head and waited. He sensed the time had come when the Beothuk was going to reveal what had happened to him. He was right. The Beothuk and the Mi'kmaq conversed in their own languages, which were similar, and by using sign language unique to their kind.

When Kop had finished telling the Mi'kmaq chief about the shooting of his wife and daughter, Jimijon said, "The man with the fiery hair was a cruel one. He is mourned by no one. The whites went back for his gun. They left his bloody head on the beach. Still they hunt you. Your head on a pole would be great token for the whites. Some wish all Beothuk were dead. Others, who say there are few Beothuk left, are trying to save you. We have seen no one but you. Maybe you are the last Beothuk."

"On the trail of my people I see only the footprints of the Unwanted Ones," said Kop. "Our *mamateeks* are as empty as our weirs. They control all the waters which run into the Great Sea. Our traplines are not respected. They steal from us without sharing with us. Still they fear us. The Mi'kmaq have aided them. This I have seen. You wear their skins and carry their death sticks."

"It is so," Jimijon said evenly. "We trade skins for food and hunting tools. We survive. For long time past my people trapped west and left you to trap east. Change comes. The whites are many, and you are few."

"When you paddled over the western sea to our land you call Ktaqamk, we too were many. Though you did not see us, we were here. We are True Born, and you too are intruders on our land."

"This too is so," said the Mi'kmaq chief, his voice as matter-of-fact and stoic as before. He used the gun as a staff to get to his feet, and when he stood looking down at Kop, he said, "We leave for the coast with the new dawn to trade our winter furs." It was his way of saying farewell.

"I will stay and search for my people," replied Kop.

Jimijon nodded, already knowing, and said, "There is always meat at my campfire for the true hunter."

"Next time the hunter will bring meat," said Kop.

The next morning, with the rose of dawn streaking across the eastern sky, the Mi'kmaq broke camp and left for the coast. And Kop was alone again.

19

HE HEARD THEM coming long before he saw them. He was downstream, more than a day's walk from the mouth of the great river which flows out of the heart of the Island of New-foundland. This river valley, where he knew the Unwanted Ones frequented, was not where he wanted to be. It was also the long-trodden ways of his ancestors. And if any of his people were left, it was likely here he would find them. So far he had found nothing but old tracks.

The time of new life had come. Leafed trees were full and gently swaying. Bushes bloomed. Birds were nesting, and the forest was fragrant. He had followed a tributary which merged with the flow of the great river beneath a huge cut bank of gravelly soil, at a point where the river bent to the southwest before entering the bay. He was standing on the very tip of the bend, drinking water at the tributary's confluence with the river and the distant bay, when he heard them.

The Unwanted Ones were coming down the river.

He heard the knock and scrape of their oars against the gunnels of their heavy boats. Their travel was loud, and their voices were louder. Kop climbed up into the shadowed forest crowded with tall timber and waited for them. Below him, eddies swirled and tucked back under the riverbanks. The lower tips of bushes bent with the pull of the water, their trunks submerged in the water. Driftwood floated by. A slight breeze meandered through the valley. It stirred the low sedges, but so subtle was the wind, the sound of it could have been the river's song.

The boat came in sight around the bend, and the handlers turned it in to the eddy below the point where Kop was hiding. There were four men with oars and a fifth who sat in the stern, a steering stick cradled under his left arm. They were rough-looking men who had journeyed far. In the centre of the boat sat a sixth person, covered with a shawl, who held no oar. Kop couldn't tell if it was a man or a woman. The one in the stern stood, stick in hand, and shouted a command. The oarsmen shipped their oars over the side. The stickman pushed hard over. The boat veered into the back eddy. With the current against its stern, it turned until its bow slowed and was pointed upstream below the bank, directly below the watching Beothuk.

The figure that sat alone in the centre of the boat shrugged its shoulders. The shawl dropped, and the face stared up with a longing expression into the woods, as if knowing Kop was watching. It wasn't a man, but a Beothuk woman! Kop almost moved from concealment, so great was his surprise and overwhelming joy at seeing one of his own kind. But past experience with the Unwanted Ones prevailed, and he remained hidden. He stared at the woman. The loosened shawl revealed long, black tresses surrounding a face with soft brown skin. She had once been beautiful to look upon. Her eyes, looking up, betrayed her beauty. They were sad and filled with despair. She was thin and haggard. The shawl she wore was draped over narrow shoulders. Her eyes had witnessed a supreme tragedy.

Presently, she lowered her head and picked up the hem of the shawl with both hands. Her hands were bound. The woman kept her eyes focused on the forest, as if expecting some ancient spirit to come by and whisk her away from the clutches of her captors.

Kop suddenly realized he had seen the woman before. She had been much younger then. Memories of feasting and merriment on the shores of the Big Red Pond on a night filled with moonlight came to him. It was the same woman. He was sure of it, though he wasn't sure of her name. But what was a Beothuk woman doing floating down the great river in the Unwanted Ones' clumsy boat? Her bonds gave him the answer. The Beothuk woman was a captive.

The men ate food from a dirty pack and tossed the Beothuk woman the scraps, which fell in her lap. After they had eaten, a shout from the stickman roused them, and they dipped their oars again. The boat turned into the current, gained way, and went slipping by the shoreline. And moving through the forest, Kop followed its passage.

The boat was edging out into the current and would soon outpace him. Kop could not resist. He called out loudly, in the Beothuk tongue, his voice ringing out over the estuary, "Are you Shanawdithit?"

When his cry rang out, the men in the boat stopped their rowing in mid-stroke and scrambled for their muskets. Their oars fell in the slack of the thole-pins and dragged sluggishly in the brown water. They pointed their muskets upwards. The stickman let go, and the boat swung broadside to the current. The men saw no one.

The woman stood to her feet in astonishment at hearing her own language come from the woods. Her eyes filled with tears, and in a voice choked with emotion she shouted back,

"Yes, I am Shanawdithit! Who is calling me from the forest that I love?"

"I am Kop, mate of Tehonee and father of Kuise, who were slain by the death sticks of the Unwanted Ones! Where can I find the others, and why are you drifting bound and alone down the great river?"

"The others are no more! They have gone *winum*. All *winum*, I think. I have heard of you. The Unwanted Ones will give many of their fire sticks for you. I have run before. I am good swimmer. This they know. Now they have tied me."

The boat shifted with the current. Shanawdithit tilted to keep her balance, and the men cursed at the voice issuing from the woods. They shouted to each other and pointed their guns. They were expecting to see a flurry of arrows fluted at them any minute.

Kop was standing with arrow nocked and bow drawn. He knew he could easily kill two of them before the current could take them out of range. But the lone Beothuk wanted something more than killing. He wanted to converse with the last of his breed. He shouted again, "Not all *winum*! Not Nonosbawsut, the tall one, fearless and mightiest of warriors!"

"Nonosbawsut, the tall one, was killed long since by the Unwanted Ones on the ice of the Great Red Pond. He was defending Demasduit, his mate, who was taken. Demasduit is gone *winum*."

The news shook Kop to the core. Nonosbawsut was a noble warrior and great hunter who had trained Buka.

The whites in the boat were uneasy. They would soon pull away, and he wanted more information from Shanawdithit.

"Where are they taking you? Where can I find more of our breed?"

"They are taking me on a ship with billowing wings, which will bear me south over the wide sea, to where I know not. Our breed is no more. I fear you are the last *osa'yan'a!*"

The men in the boat had relaxed some, after no arrows came and they felt sure there was only one man watching them. But they still kept their guns pointed toward Kop's voice, and they were still wary. But seeing no threat, the stickman gave a command. Two of the men put down their guns and took up the oars, while the other two kept their guns pointed shoreward. With the first stroke of the oars, the boat pulled away from the shore.

Both Kop and Shanawdithit knew their voices would soon be silenced with distance. Shanawdithit cried out, "Search for them! In the hidden valleys beneath the mountains. In the deepest forest you may yet find them."

She was about to say more, when a blow from one of the oarsmen racked her head sideways. She slumped down on the middle thwart and was still. The Unwanted Ones had heard enough of the savage prattle. The boat took the surge of the current and veered away, out of arrow range.

Kop shouted after them, "I will search for them down every trail! Beneath high mountains where green valleys make way, I will seek them. And though their spirits, like rivers, are forever hidden in the Great Sea, still I will search for them."

THE BEOTHUK SEASONS passed and five of the Unwanted Ones' years went by, and in all that time Kop found no trace of his own kind. He was now truly the last Beothuk. The small Mi'kmaq Bear Clan grew to both accept and ignore the Beothuk who sometimes appeared in their camp. He always appeared when the evening fire was low. And the hunter always brought welcomed meat for Jimijon's spit. The Mi'kmaq were as nomadic as the Beothuk. They followed the caribou migrations across the island. They trapped the interior during the fall and winter, and they fished on the coast in the spring and summer. The vast hunting grounds surrounding what the Unwanted Ones called Red Indian Lake were being explored and hunted extensively. Forays into its regions by the whites to hunt the Beothuk had begun. To capture them. To save them. All failed. And when no retaliation came from the Red Indian lands, the slaughter of deer began.

WEALTHY ENGLISHMEN WERE experienced in hunting from the green veldts of central Africa to the endless plains of Tanzania's Serengeti. They offered purses, heavy with the coin of the British realm, to English outfitters, to be taken on safaris of slaughter. The sweating backs of black bondsmen, slaves and guides, suffered under packs of food and drink of which they would never partake. Their hunting treks were long and winding and brutally fruitful.

Stories of other buffaloes, in countless numbers, circulated around the English gentry. And they came to the American plains to hunt. To test the deadly ability of new rifles. To kill. To destroy. And to enslave. Upon their manor walls hung the curved horns of Africa's mighty cape buffalo. The draped robes of the disappearing American bison. The black tresses of the Red Indian.

And then tales of a virgin wilderness, where caribou as tame as English pups and sporting magnificent broad antlers, came from ships returning laden with riches. No one hunted them save for savage heathens with primitive bow and arrow. The English sportsmen sailed to Newfoundland to hunt caribou and any other wild creature they encountered. And when they went hunting, the Mi'kmaq led them. They carried out only the best of antlered racks. They left behind the rotting carcasses of hundreds of slain deer.

"We only guide the English. We do not kill for them. And though the Beothuk trail is cold, we do not lead them there," Jimijon said one night when Kop had confronted him about leading the Unwanted Ones on hunting sprees for caribou.

"The *kosweet*, like the Beothuk, were once many. Now they are few," said Kop, and he said no more.

Despite their arguments, Kop and Jimijon remained friends, at arm's length. For the most part, though their way of life was rapidly changing, the Mi'kmaq still hung on to their old ways. Trading furs was an age-old tradition with them. For the Beothuk, it was not.

Kop still kept to the old trapping grounds of the Beothuk. The tributaries north and west of Red Indian Lake were still largely untouched. When he came across the steel traps of the whites, he destroyed them. He was adept at trapping the marten cat. The animal, when cured properly, boasted the richest of furs on the Island of Newfoundland. He left their soft hides, as well as the cured hides of fox, otter, and beaver, with the Bear Clan. The Mi'kmaq continued their trading with the people they called Europeans. They traded with the English, whom Jimijon told Kop had cheated them. They preferred to deal with the French traders on the west coast of the Island rather than with the English. He said the English trader wanted pelts piled as high as a gun was long before he would even talk trade. The French would trade for furs half the gun's height, providing they were all otter and marten cat fur. Powder and shot could be traded for lesser furs.

EARLY ONE SPRING, when the clan left the hunting grounds and walked west, Kop went with them. The trapping season had been good, and they carried furs upon their backs or dragged sleds filled with furs behind them. The Beothuk had not stained his skin red since Kuise's death. His skin colour had a softer, richer hue than the others, but he blended well with the Mi'kmaq.

Kop kept back while Jimijon traded with the Frenchman on the steps of his trading post. There were other Europeans present. They resented the Mi'kmaq collection of furs. They never mingled with them and rarely said more than curse words to them. They never once suspected the last Beothuk was standing near them. If you saw one Indian, you had seen them all, they believed. And the Mi'kmaq did not betray the Beothuk.

Though Jimijon had informed Kop he could barter for a gun for himself in exchange for the marten pelts, Kop refused. He wanted nothing to do with the weapon which had caused him so much pain. Which had destroyed his world. He would not wear the white man's garb nor use his traps of steel. He did accept a knife and a small kettle. The only items Kop cherished from the whites were the coarse, sand-like sugar and tea. He loved the sweet taste of the earth-coloured liquid. He would accept nothing more from the Unwanted Ones' way. From Jimijon he learned of the happenings in his land. Jimijon could get by with both the French and English languages, though neither the English nor the French tried to learn his. Jimijon informed Kop of coastal events, and Kop told him what he saw inland.

ON ONE OF his trips to Notre Dame Bay, Jimijon learned from a servant who was "in service" to John Peyton the younger, in whose home Shanawdithit spent most of her last days, that the woman had been carried away to St. John's to be placed on public display. There she fell ill with the coughing sickness so prevalent among the Europeans. The Beothuk had no resistance whatsoever against the dreaded disease. The white healers could not save her, and there she died on a Saturday night, June 29, 1829, far away from the hills where she had lived.

Kop's demeanour changed with the news. His face was etched with a terrible loneliness borne from the soul, such as no one could ever know. He looked into the surrounding forest at the edge of where he and Jimijon were seated by a campfire. Night had come, and the forest was dark and still. For Kop it was now truly empty and bereft of life. The silence went on between the two men.

Then Kop wondered aloud if the bearer of such news had told how and where Shanawdithit had been buried. Jimijon was silent for the longest time and avoided Kop's eyes. Kop sensed the Mi'kmaq knew more. After a while, the Mi'kmaq gave him his answer.

The body of the last Beothuk woman had been disembowelled by curious St. John's doctors. By doing so, they were not looking to determine how the woman had died. They already knew that. What they were so keen on learning was whether or not Shanawdithit was, "in form and feature, face and limb," the same as other human women. Her remains were not permitted to be laid in the same hallowed burial ground with European people. She was laid to rest, without ceremony, in an obscure piece of ground: headless, unmourned, unsung, unmarked.

Kop didn't speak for a long time after hearing this. The fire was nursed into small flames. Something rustled among the leaves somewhere in the woods. Both men looked up, but the sound didn't come again.

"I have seen the burial boxes of the Unwanted Ones many seasons ago," Kop said suddenly. And he in turn told Jimijon what he had once seen by the shores of Red Indian Lake. He never went to stay there anymore, he said. Not even for one day or night. But his trail frequently led him past the area of his birth, where the black openings of the empty lodges stared at him. It was one of these openings which had halted him one day. The lodge doorway was closed. Not only was it closed, but it was sewn tight, from the outside.

A single wide piece of birchbark, white as new snow, had been carefully stitched with leather lacings to the stud frame of the *mamateek*. Kop did not need to go closer to investigate what it meant. He knew. The smoke hole had been closed to keep the spirits of the dead safe within. The lodge had been used as a burial site by one of his kind. He was more interested in the trail of the living, but their trail of life was as cold as their trail of death. Their footprints were hidden beneath autumn leaves.

Long after, when he came by the same trail, he slowed yet again. The birchbark had only slightly faded. But the doorway had been cut open.

Someone with no respect had dared to enter the sanctuary of the dead. Strong winds were blowing that day. The trees were moving with the might of it. The lake surface was a seething white disturbance. Kop ventured forward just enough to peer inside. He was afraid and would go no farther. What he saw in the dim light was a crude platform above the lodge floor. He was astonished to see placed on it a wooden coffin built by the Unwanted Ones. A coffin stained red. There were three bodies. On one side of the coffin were the remains of a body wrapped in birchbark. It was as tall as the coffin beside it. On the other side of the coffin was a smaller body, also wrapped. The coffin as well as both death shrouds had been cut away. All three of the dead were stained as red as the wooden tomb. The two adults were headless. Kop was terrified and fled. And the spirits of the dead, borne by the hissing wind, chased him.

Even now, long after, Kop was very upset by what he had seen, and the telling of it unnerved him. He told Jimijon he knew not who the dead were. Jimijon pulled a clay pipe from the deep pocket of his European-made coat. He tapped the dottle out and tamped the bowl tight with coarse, dark tobacco using a broad thumb whose dirty nail was stubbed and broken. From the small woodpile he found a split, and lighting it from the fire coals, he brought it to the pipe bowl. The pipe flared, and smoke escaped from one corner of his mouth. He sucked again and inhaled. A cloud of heady smoke spilled out of his nostrils and mouth. Satisfied the pipe was drawing well, Jimijon pulled it from his mouth, spat into the fire, glanced sideways at Kop, and said, "The names of the dead have been whispered to me."

Kop stared at him and waited. He knew Jimijon well enough to know the man would not be rushed. The chief puffed from the pipe again as if considering how to continue. What he had to tell Kop was not pleasant.

"The one the whites call Cormack is like you," he began. Kop's black eyes narrowed and bore into Jimijon's face.

"He, too, searched for the Beothuk on empty trails," Jimijon said quickly.

Kop didn't fully understand, but his expression relaxed some.

"The one the whites call Joe Sylvester guided him many seasons past. Joe, like me, was Mi'kmaq. He was a good guide. Not a good hunter. He was a bit lazy, too. He was afraid of the red devils." Jimijon shot a look at the "red devil" sitting next to him. Kop took no notice of the slur.

"Joe took Cormack down the valleys where the Beothuk were not."

"We watched them go by. We didn't want to be found," said Kop.

Jimijon glanced at him and nodded. "When Joe led Cormack to the far western bay, to what my people call Noywa'Mkisk—where the sand blows—Cormack's ribs were showing. He was sore from the bites of the no-see-ums and his spirit was barren, but his pride was great. He was the first of the whites to cross this land they say is an island."

"Our land is surrounded by the salt sea," said Kop, confirming the statement. Jimijon nodded again.

"Seasons went by. Cormack returned. He was still searching for the Beothuk. He needed good guides, all Indian.

"One Mi'kmaq, one Abenaki, and one mountaineer guided him up the great river to the Red Pond. They found the lodge you speak of. The one with the door sewn tight. The guides feared the death spirits of the red man. Cormack did not." Jimijon paused long enough for Kop to think he had finished, when he spoke again. His voice was low.

"In the wooden box made by the whites was the body of the one you call Nonosbawsut, the tall one. He was murdered defending his woman. Lying with him was his woman, Demasduit, the one the whites call Mary March. She was carried there by the whites after she died of the white man's sickness. Nonosbawsut was put there after by the Beothuk. Their child, too, who had died soon after the mother, was taken away and placed in the lodge. Cormack cut through the opening and went inside."

Jimijon paused again. Kop could tell he did not want to speak. He also knew what he was going to tell him.

"Speak," he told the Mi'kmaq. It was more of a plea than a request. And after a time, Jimijon continued.

"Cormack cut the heads from Demasduit and Nonosbawsut." The words spilled out of his mouth like bile he wanted to be rid of. "He carried them away in his pack," he finished.

Kop gasped at the revelation. Though he knew what was coming, the truth of it was no less disturbing. The burial grounds of his people had been desecrated, dishonoured by the very ones who had caused all three deaths. How were his people to enter the spirit world without their heads?

Did they hold nothing sacred? They were worse than animals. Even in death, the True People were hunted by the Unwanted Ones.

He and Jimijon talked for a short time about the dishonour which had been committed. Then Jimijon told Kop that Cormack's guides, too, were appalled by what the white man had done. They showed their disgust for his foul deed on the trip back down the Exploits to the coast. They seldom hunted for food, rarely spoke to Cormack, and as he grew weak from hunger and fatigue, they offered him little assistance. When they arrived back to the coast, Cormack was near death, but he survived.

"He lives still?" asked Kop.

"Though he has crossed the Great Sea to the land where only whites live, it is so. He carried the stolen heads with him."

THE MI'KMAQ CHIEF's telling of the abused remains of the last of his people disturbed the Beothuk greatly. Kop had nightmares about his people searching, without heads, for the death spirits. He had been taught the spirits of the dead guided them to the afterworld. Now he wasn't sure if the spirits had left with the severed heads or had remained with the headless bodies. He remembered that he had removed the head from the red-headed one so that he would not see his spirit world. It disturbed him greatly.

He had stopped wearing the red ochre and no longer felt a spiritual presence. Kop had given up on his ancient religion. The disturbing story reminded him of something he had to do. He left for the coast and journeyed alone to the place where the bones of his only descendant were buried. He carried red ochre in a pouch of intricate leather. Kuise's burial site had not been disturbed. Even the animals had merely sniffed at the raised mound and left without disturbing it. Only the Unwanted Ones disturbed the sleep of the dead. Kop's disdain for them grew.

It took him several hours to complete the burial ritual on his daughter's remains. Kuise's spirit was her own and not his. And though he no longer wore the red ochre, he would honour his daughter's spirit. He painted her entire skeleton. He stained what was left of her clothing. He painted her swaddling bark. And when he had done all of that, Kop smeared the sacred ground above his Small One with the last of the dye.

20

AFTER THEY HAD lost their fear of him, the Mi'kmaq women of the Bear Clan admired the tall Beothuk who came frequently into their camp. There were only two younger ones of mating years. One was short and giggled a lot when he was around. She had eyes for Kop. But a strong Mi'kmaq, young, a good hunter and provider who was a much-respected member of the band, also had eyes for her.

The other one was tall and taut as a young pine and in her first blood years. She, too, cast her brown eyes for the Beothuk. For the longest time Kop ignored both of them. The short one soon lost interest in Kop and mated with the Mi'kmaq hunter.

Then one day, Kop noticed the other for the first time. As a man sees a woman. She had cast her eyes his way again, and seeing his disinterest, she was walking away from him when Kop looked after her. The girl's hips, nubile and daring, moved in time with her every move. Kop's loins stirred for the first time since Tehonee's death. Two nights after that, Kop's mind was on mating.

It was the time of trees greening. The Bear Clan had come to the bay named for the English saint George to trade furs, and Kop had come down the trail with them. The trapping season had not been a good one. Deep snow and bitter winds had prevailed. Fur-bearing animals had kept hidden. Only Kop, with his prime catch of pine marten, had done well. He shared his hides with the Bear Clan, and Jimijon traded for food and ammunition. The apprentice running the trading post in his master's absence had assured him the prices offered were fair ones. The fur trade in Europe was not a demanding one just now, he told Jimijon. Canadian beaver and American buffalo hides had glutted the European market. Jimijon merely stared at the apprentice, understanding only that the pile of furs on the wooden counter brought from a wilderness of untold hardship was not enough. Still, that evening, on a grassy knoll beside a brook at the wide mouth of the bay where they had made camp, they feasted on the white man's food and drink.

A bottle of brown liquid was passed around to drink. When it was offered to Kop, his nostrils flared in disgust, and he would not drink. The night was one of revelry. Home from the winter hills, the Mi'kmaq were celebrating. Stories of the hunt were told before a blazing campfire, and the lean time of cold was forgotten. The setting sun drew shadows over the mountains.

Her name was Isadore Quam'uit. When Kop asked her what her name meant, she said she didn't know. Kop was amazed to hear her name had no meaning. Everyone in the camp called her Isa. They were sitting outside the fragmented light rim of the campfire. Night had come, soft and warm. Songbirds sang and twittered. The wobbling pitch of the hunting snipe above and the plaintive call of a pair of loons on the bay below charmed the air with melodious night sounds. A full yellow moon came stealing up over the treetops.

Laughing voices behind them echoed across the night water. Isa was sitting beside Kop on the meadow. Her knees were drawn up, and her slim brown arms were cradled over them. Between her short moccasins and the buckskin hem of her dress, her smooth calves were washed with the silvery light of the night orb. Isa came willingly into Kop's arms, her beating heart filled with love. Kop's eyes held only lust. When he took her, her naked skin was soft, brown, and polished with moonlight. She was innocent to all of it. The girl cried out, and then the woman moaned.

Kop and Isa blended their bodies for many days and more wondrous nights. Isa was doe-eyed and loving, while Kop was carnal. Then one day, the Mi'kmaq decided to journey south by the coast to pursue their way of life. Kop went north and east into the mountain valleys. He did not take Isa with him. The time of leaves falling came again. The Bear Clan trekked away from the sea and made their way through the traces beneath the rims of the flat-topped mountains. One day when the snow had come and the water was ice, Kop came striding into their camp. Across his shoulders he carried a fat doe caribou. Once again, the hunter had brought meat to the campfire of the Bear Clan. Isa, her belly swollen, walked shyly toward her lover. Kop said, "I will build a berthing lodge." It was his only acknowledgement of Isa's condition.

THE LONG TIME of cold was easing. Days were longer. The snow melt had begun. On a night that was warm with the promise of spring, Isa's cries began. A woman only a few seasons older than Isa but who had endured the birth pains of two sons was with her. Kop was seated with the others of the clan outside by a communal campfire. The lodge Kop had built for himself and Isa was on the far side of the clearing. It was not far enough to mask the pains of birth. Isa's screams went on and on. Kop tended the fire until the glow of it was hidden by the new day.

And when the rising sun had cleared the lip of the mountains, Isa's cries were muted by the wail of new life. Kop had fallen asleep by the dying fire and did not hear it.

Isa asked Kop if he was going to smear their girl-child with the red clay. He thought for a while, remembering another infant girl whose skin had still borne the birth scent of her mother when he had stained her. From Tehonee's belly had come the last true Beothuk. Kuise, his Small One, was pureborn and deserving of the red earth sacred and unique to the Beothuk. Kop would not anoint one of mixed blood. He told Isa no. She understood little of the Beothuk language. She asked with words and signs what he wanted the child to be called. Kop understood her meaning.

"She is *emamoosatu*," he said. Isa fumbled with the word, not pronouncing it properly.

"Santu," Isa stammered the last of the word, trying to get it right. And Kop, thinking it was the name she wanted, and not really caring, agreed with her.

"We will call her Santu," he said.

KOP CONTINUED TO spend time with the Bear Clan, feeling an obligation toward Isa, who willingly shared his sleeping mat, and now especially toward Santu, who had her father's black eyes and was rapidly growing Kop's bear-like mane. Kop always hunted and trapped alone. But when he came to their camp, he shared with all. Santu grew quickly. From her father she learned the Beothuk ways and to speak only some of his language. Kop was not much of a talker. And though he often entered Jimijon's camp, he was still a loner. Santu grew up hard.

For the Indians, both the Mi'kmaq and the lone Beothuk who spent time in their midst, the Unwanted Ones' encroachment had changed a way of life forever. For the Mi'kmaq it meant bending with the surge of wind that had come among them, and because they were willing to bend, they would survive. But they were treated with the same disdain the Unwanted Ones showed for the Beothuk. The wealth of their traditional land and water was denied them, for the most part. The Europeans dealt with the Mi'kmaq only at arm's length and exploited their expertise of the wilderness. And the Mi'kmaq were bent into service. For Kop, the last true Beothuk, who would not bend, it was too late.

Then one autumn, after the Bear Clan had done their spring trading and finished with summer wanderings on the west coast and were beginning their annual trek back to their wintering grounds, Isa started coughing.

Kop was not with them, and young Santu carried her mother's load. When the time for deep snows had come and the long nights of cold had settled upon the land, Kop joined the Mi'kmaq again. Now when Isa coughed, which was often, there was a yellow fluid flecked with blood in her sputum.

There was another in the camp who shared the same symptoms. It was a woman of many years. Her breathing was laboured, shallow, and brought blood to the corners of her mouth. Her weary bones framed her gaunt features. Her fingers were claw-like. She drank only a grey broth fed to her by one of her daughters. The old woman was dying. The Bear Clan had brought consumption into their camp.

Bending down, Kop drew the door flap open and entered the wigwam where Isa lay with closed eyes. Smoke rose slowly from the campfire inside. The smoke hole was not open wide enough, and some of the smoke remained inside. Meat and fish hung from the drying rack. The lodge was dismal and uninviting. Isa was lying on her side on a mattress of boughs. The stems of the boughs were bare in places and had lost most of their cushion. She tried to turn when Kop bent down to her, and she opened her eyes. The youth had gone from her face. Her hair was greasy and knotted and had not been combed.

Isa reached up, and Kop took both her hands in his. A retching cough overwhelmed the young woman. She drew a hand from Kop's to cover her mouth, and blood appeared between her fingers. A woman who had been watching came out of the shadows. She gently removed Isa's hand from her mouth. With a piece of cloth stained with blood and crusted with mucus, she wiped fresh blood from Isa's mouth. In doing so, she smeared blood across Isa's brown skin. Isa returned her hand to Kop's. It was hot and sticky with her blood. Kop knew her death spirit was waiting. It would not be a long wait.

Isa died two days before the old woman. The Bear Clan dug two holes beneath the snow in a gravelly bank above the white frozen side of a stream whose middle flowed with black winter water. The old woman was laid down in one, and Isa was placed in the other. The bodies were buried face up without burial coverings. They began to fill in the hole with the soil they had dug out. They covered the feet first. Santu was standing by her father, watching in silence. When all that was left uncovered was the face of the only one who had ever loved her, Santu cried aloud. Kop showed no emotion. Tears filled Santu's eyes, and she clung to her father's hand. Her hands were warm. Full of life. Kop squeezed them back. With tears rolling down her cheeks, Santu looked up in surprise. For the first time, her father was showing her affection.

Kop's mind was reeling. Not with grief, but with frustration. All that he had had been taken from him by the Unwanted Ones. His parents. His beloved Tehonee and the child of their love. And now Isa had died from a mysterious illness unknown to them, as invisible as the lead ball thrown from the thunder sticks. His entire world had been destroyed by the Unwanted Ones. He saw in the hole carved out of the winter ground two more bodies. They had been wrapped in soft white bark and did not see the soil come tumbling down upon them. By their side were their most prized possessions. And they were painted with red ochre, so they could enter the spirit world with pride.

Kop wished he had red ochre. Even though she was not Beothuk, Isa had loved him as much as Tehonee had, and he would have anointed her with the red earth. But he had given up on the spirits, and in his pack there was no sacred red clay. The feeling passed, and Kop helped the others fill in Isa's grave before leaving the site. When they walked away, Santu held his hand.

THE WINTER PASSED slowly. Spring warmth came, and before the strength went out of the snow, the Bear Clan left again for St. George's Bay on Newfoundland's west coast to barter their furs. Kop journeyed with them. As was his wont, he did not enter the mercantile store where Jimijon traded but sat watching from the trees nearby. The spring sun was warm, and he swatted at flies that had found him. Soon Jimijon came out of the ramshackle trading post and found Kop.

"We are going away from this place." Kop, who knew Jimijon well, knew he didn't mean that he was leaving to fish by the coastal waters.

"Where?" he asked, accepting the small sack of brown sugar Jimijon offered him. The bag of sugar, one bag of strong tea leaves, and two blankets, one of which moths had found, was his trade for the full winter's catch of pine marten. Kop eyed the supplies and said nothing.

"Across the Great Water to the land of our ancestors."

Kop looked up in surprise. "In the ships of the Unwanted Ones?"

"No. We will paddle in our own sea canoes, as we have always done."

"The hardest paddle is out to the mighty current stronger than the great river. It will carry you to the small island near the big land, which goes forever west."

"You know of this tide and the endless land beyond?" It was Jimijon's turn to be surprised.

Kop merely nodded. "My people, too, paddled to and fro over that same *ebautho*. Looking from the high mountains, they could see the distant land. With only two hands of sun left, they watched small birds that don't land on water or fly at night fly out over the sea. And sometimes before a storm, the storm spirits loomed over the land high enough above the sea for all to see. When the south wind had brought all of its warmth to us and stopped blowing, they paddled out to the great current. Even the whale's spirit watched them. Rising beside them at night, its big eye glinting with moonlight showed them the way."

"It is so," said Jimijon. The Mi'kmaq knew the crossing well.

"When will you leave?"

"As your people did, when the south winds have quieted."

"All of you?"

"No. Only some of us. In three boats."

"Take Santu with you."

"You will still search?"

"I will search till I die."

"There is a place my people call Miawpukek. It is miles from the open sea, at the end of a long saltwater lake surrounded by mountains. There are rivers filled with fat trout and salmon. Caribou roam the barrens, and the whites do not go there. My people are finding refuge from the whites there. Maybe there is a Beothuk with them. A woman." Jimijon ended with a grin.

"Maybe it is so."

"The whites have bred with our women. Not all of them were willing. Some of our young bucks have lain with white women, too. All of them were willing. Maybe there is already Beothuk blood among your Unwanted Ones!"

Kop stared at Jimijon long and considered such a thing before he answered.

"Maybe this, too, is so," he said. His voice was low, as if he did not want to think of such a thing.

"YOU CARRY THE blood of two races in your veins," Kop said after he informed Santu he wanted her to leave with the Bear Clan.

"My blood is my own." Santu spoke harshly, but her head was bowed.

Kop wasn't expecting such wisdom from her and wasn't sure how to continue. But he tried.

"This is so. But you alone carry the woman spirit of Tehonee and Kuise and Isa. Though your blood is yours, it flows with the spirit of others. My spirit, which you carry, is like the sun, which is already down in the west. Only its glow remains. Soon that light, too, is a memory. The spirit of Isa, she who gave you life, is like the promise of a glowing dawn within you. The Mi'kmaq are many. Their spirit will go on. And they will care for you. I am alone, the last of my breed. My spirit will die searching. And for you I choose a different life."

Kop faced the distant hills, already knowing where he would go.

"I do not want to leave. But I will go," Santu answered with a determination she did not feel. She reached for her father's hand. Kop took it in hers and squeezed. The night had come. Stars glittered, and the moon path was already showing on the bay.

"If I return, where will I find you?" she asked quietly.

Kop looked at the moonlight on the water, at the skies filled with starshine, at the dark forest behind him.

"You will find me where I have always been."

When Santu was roused from her sleep the next morning by the clamour of a breaking camp, she hurried outside the lodge. There was no wind. The skies were clear and bright. And Kop was gone.

Epilogue

My name in my own tongue is Kopituk, from the beaver root, out of which my father squeezed the red juice onto my brown skin, while the life vine from my mother's belly still dangled from mine. I am also called Kop. My heart is wrapped in stone till I learn how it beats.

From the time before time, we were here. And you were not. Yet when you came here you "discovered" our Island. Passed down to us from a thousand campfires and carried over a thousand trails by our Mages are the stories of others like you, who came here from out of the sea where the sun awakens. Their ships were also carried by wings. And when the wind spirits forsook them and the sea was calm, they made their way with long oars protruding from the ship sides. They, too, discovered us and settled on the northernmost reaches of our Island without asking permission. They were a fierce tribe of marauders who lived in earthen mounds like bears and strayed only short distances from them. We harried them without cease. And after a time, they left and did not return.

Now you, fiercest of all marauders, have come from over the same sea in numbers far greater than the others. In every mouth of every river, where fish in plenty for all come home from the sea to multiply, you kill until the current is red with their blood. From the Great Sea you scoop fishes as plentiful as stars. And beyond the rim of our salty shore you take furs far more than you can ever wear. You kill more meat than you can ever eat. The maggots grow fat with the waste. The raven is too bloated to fly. And still you are not satisfied.

This and much more my people determined from the veils of trees through which we peered. Futile attempts to placate us, and not to ask permission for the harvest you claimed as your own, ended in betrayal and death by your hand. Always by the sea, rich with life and on the banks of our rivers of wealth, you did dwell. Your presence brought death and poverty to my race. I rebelled. Against my parents. Against the elders. I was young, virile, and invincible.

I retreated into the vast interior of the greatest of islands, where you had not the courage to venture. With me went my willing mate. Her spirit name was Tehobosheen, which means morning star and one who warms. I called her Tehonee, which means warm star. She was as lovely to look upon as an autumn sunset. She was as full of life as a fast-flowing stream. Her eyes were as limpid as a starry winter sky, and her smile, warm as spring sunlight on melting snow, was only for me. We fumbled through sweet nights of ecstatic revelations. Upon soft cushions of green moss and in clear pools of revealing water, we sought and found mutual pleasure. Before the long, cold nights had come and without knowing we were searching, we had discovered love. And in the spring, when the sun brought new life to the land, the longing of our lovemaking brought forth our own new life. We gave her her own spirit name, Kuis-duit, for the sun and the flowers which grow by the lake. We called her Small One, or Kuise.

I led my small family back to the shores of plenty, by the

Great Sea, following the way of my ancestors. I hid by the side of our trails disturbed by your booted feet. Your hated scent and your loud clamour raced ahead of you. I was as silent as the lone star which dogs the moon. My scent was of the earth. You did not see or hear me. But I saw you. And I witnessed your vile deeds.

To the coasts of plenty, I am denied. There you shoot at me with your death sticks which roar like *baradirsick*.

I no longer burnish my skin with the sacred red dye, fearing recognition. Now I blend with the others of a similar race. I am alone in a crowd.

We take trinkets you have left unguarded, and you call us thieves. You have stolen our greatest possession—our way of life, our land and all of its riches—yet they call you great discoverers and merchants of fortune. You kill because we are different, and you are lauded as great hunters. We kill in defence and are called murderers. You take without asking all there is to take.

From me you have stolen the very reason for life: my parents, my mate, my child. All have fallen, to rise no more, before the noise of your guns. Many of my friends, too, have died when your guns spoke. And my new lover was taken from me by the foul spore issued out of your breath. And still you keep on taking what is not yours to take.

For the others who share my skin colour—the Mi'kmaq, around whose campfire I found peace and with whom I have walked—you also have changed a way of life. You treat them little better than your dogs. But they are like a tall pine which bends to the might of the storm. And because they bend, they will survive. My people are like the rock in the gale, which only time can change. You would not give us that time. And when you could not bend us, you broke us.

Now I alone remain. You, who are many, do not know alone. Alone is a path where there are no footprints. Alone is a cold black window with no light shining through. Alone is cold ashes. Alone is emptiness.

Give back the bones of my people.

You are the Unwanted Ones.

Afterword

This book is a work of historical fiction. Most of the characters represented are real people. Others I have created. Shanawdithit, believed by many to be the last of the Beothuk, was a real person, as was Demasduit and her husband, Nonosbawsut. Santu was also a real person. As real as her father, Kop. I believe Kop was the last pure Beothuk. This of course requires an explanation.

Frank Gouldsmith Speck was an American and one of the most respected anthropologists and ethnographers of his time. Speck specialized in the Algonquin and Iroquois peoples of the eastern woodlands of North America, as well as in the indigenous peoples of eastern boreal Canada. He was especially interested in the vanished race of Indians of Newfoundland—the Beothuk. Speck was doubtful that an entire breed of people could be erased without one trace. Amazingly, he found—while conversing with a family of Mi'kmaq he assumed were American—evidence to back up his supposition in July of 1910 in Gloucester, Massachusetts.

The native family consisted of an aged woman, her son, his wife, and child. The old woman could not speak English. Her son spoke both Mi'kmaq and English. He translated for

Speck and his mother. When Speck asked where she had been born, the woman said she was born in Newfoundland.

"Are you Mi'kmaq?" asked Speck.

"No. Not true Mi'kmaq. My mother was Mi'kmaq. My father was Kop, called after the red root. My name is Santu."

Speck was astounded. He asked more questions. Santu told him she was born on the shores of the big "Red Pond" in Newfoundland. Through her account of events, Speck determined Santu to be about seventy-five years old. She had been born five or six years after Shanawdithit's death. This had to mean her father, Kop, was not only alive in 1829 but had lived many years after that.

Her father was born on the shores of the Red Pond, too, Santu informed Speck. He had been painted red at birth. He ate mostly raw meat. The Mi'kmaq had kidnapped Kop when he was young. According to her, her father's entire race had been "killed off" by the Europeans. Santu told Speck she had crossed over the water to Nova Scotia when she was nine or ten. She eventually married a Mohawk Indian who trapped into the Great Lakes. To escape being drafted in the civil war of 1861–65, she fled with her husband to the northeastern United States and eastern Canada, where he died.

Santu returned to Nova Scotia and married a Mi'kmaq chief whose name was Toney. She bore him five children. He treated her badly, and she eventually left him, taking her youngest son with her. When Speck interviewed Santu, she was weaving baskets by the side of a dusty road. She and her son were living hard and barely surviving.

It was Joe Toney who translated his mother's words for Speck. Santu returned to Nova Scotia, where she died. Joe Toney lived to be 101 years old, and he, too, died in Nova Scotia.

Joe Toney said his mother always told him that her father, Kop, was the last Beothuk.

Most researchers, then and now, dismissed Speck's report out of hand. He had no written documents to confirm his claim. He did not have the required three-point proof of journalism. After all, two of his points had come from talking to illiterate Indians. They were probably lying. Speck could see no reason whatsoever for Santu to lie. I share his view.

Like the story of Santu, the atrocities described in the foregoing pages are based on fact. It was not my intention to portray the Beothuk as "innocent Indians." They were not. It is true the Beothuk sometimes severed the heads of their slain enemies. They skewered them upon poles and even danced around them with glee. From hiding, they shot arrows and killed fishermen. They cut vessels from their moorings, setting them adrift. They pilfered all useful items left unattended. They were like ghosts. They applied their guerrilla warfare, but it had a limited effect. Their land and everything upon it was being taken from them, and they retaliated the only way they knew how.

But I could not find one recorded account of the Beothuk harming women or children. The same cannot be said of the European settlers.

In June 1823, two trappers were sitting beside their campfire cooking a meal. From the woods stepped a Beothuk father and his small daughter. Both natives wore animal skins which were tattered and torn. The girl's feet were bare and bleeding. Both their faces were drawn and their bones defined. They were obviously dying of starvation. The little girl held her cupped hands in front of her emaciated body, the widely accepted symbol for begging for food. The two trappers opened fire and killed both father and daughter.

Back in the community, their boasts of hunting down and killing two of the "thievin' Injuns" were met with disdain. The authorities were notified. The two trappers were summoned to court to answer for their actions. The judged deemed the trappers acted in self-defence against the "savages," and they were acquitted.

Tales of Beothuk women baring their breasts to show their sex and therefore avoid harm are well-documented. In some cases they were killed anyway. There are even stories told of trappers who notched the wooden stocks of their guns to indicate Beothuk kills. Mamateeks were burned, and one was reported to have bodies inside. It was not known how they died. Fingers and hands of the Beothuk were displayed as hunting trophies. There is no doubt stories were exaggerated, on both sides. They always are.

The story was told by trappers, who had journeyed out of the vast western wilderness of what was not yet Canada, of a deplorable act dealt to a tribe of indigenous people living there. A native trapper of one of the tribes far to the northwest, who had been trapping and trading with the English, had been given a gift by a sutler.

It had been sent from their Great Father and chief across the sea. The trapper was told that the gift was so powerful, only the chief of his tribe could open it. It was wrapped in richly coloured calico—much prized by the natives—inside a pine marten hide. He was further informed that, directly upon the gift being opened, by the chief, it must be passed to everyone in the village—men, women, and children. And to further please the Great Chief, the scent of the sacred herb within must be inhaled by all. It was like a smudging and would be a spirit bond between them.

True to his word, the trapper carried the gift deep into the interior and presented it to his chief, unopened. When the chief pulled it from the marten pelt, he found an ornate wooden box painted a deep vermilion. The box itself was a treasure to the chief. He opened it, and inside was a smaller box, and another inside that. They were all of brilliant colours and intricate in design. The last box contained what looked like a small herb or a piece of chakra found on the birch trees. Informed by the trapper that it was the wish of the English chief that he inhale the scent of the gift, the chief inhaled deeply. It smelled sweet and inviting. Then, as instructed, he passed the box around the village for all to breathe into their lungs the scent of the gift.

Two nights after that, a three-month-old baby became violently ill. She was dead before dawn. The chief died next. By now there was no one in the village well enough to build his funeral pyre. And after the chief, the trapper who had brought the deadly spore died. The remaining villagers, those who were able, fled in fear. They carried the contagion with them.

While writing this book, I wondered if my ancestors would have been one of the Beothuk's adversaries, given my British and Welsh lineage. I wonder how any of us would have treated the "savages" given the mindset of that century. If any of us born of European descent, and living a mere 150 years or so thence, did not conform to the corporal rule of the land to which we were indoctrinated . . . a hand severed for the theft of one loaf of mouldy bread; an ear lopped off for insubordination; castration for premarital sex; public flogging for not doffing a hat to passing royalty; hanging for horse theft. Yet we would have been acquitted for killing "savages."

In our modern world of inclusion and acceptance of minorities, it is not easy to imagine that we could have been some of Kop's Unwanted Ones.

I would be remiss and negligent after writing this book

if I did not include my voice and implore, along with those who are submitting to the powers that be, to have the skulls of Demasduit and her husband, Nonosbawsut, repatriated to Newfoundland, where they belong. The bones of those two Beothuk Indians are currently in a museum in Scotland.

I get some solace knowing that there is a chance—albeit a slim one—that my family tree may be blended with indigenous blood.

Acknowledgements

A special thank you to my publisher, Flanker Press, specifically Garry, Margo, and Jerry Cranford, for entrusting me with the sensitive subject matter of this work.

Thanks also to the following: Lori Temple, The Rooms, Provincial Archives Division; the Beothuk Interpretation Centre, Boyd's Cove, Newfoundland; Jeff Howard; and Robin Collins.

A special thanks to my wife, Rose.

Select Glossary

abideshhook: lynx
adjiech: two
adothe: canoe
aschautch: meat
baradirsick: thunder
be'nam: woman
bobusowet: codfish
bosdic: woodsmoke
dabseek: four
deliiue: egg
ebautho: water
edru: otter
eenodsha: hear
ejew: sea
ewinon: father
gau: rain
gu'wa: fat person
imamus: woman
kaniskwe'te: pointed hat
keathut: head
kop: red beaver root

kosweet: caribou
kuis: sun
kuisduit: a flower which grows by a lake
kuise: moon
mamateek: dwelling or birchbark shelter
mamchet: beaver
mammassmit: dog
mandzey: black
memet: hand
meotick: summer lodge
moosin: shoe
mu'ksan: boot, moccasin
munes: spirits
ninejeek: five
odemiut: ochre
obosheen: one who warms
odoit: eat
pushaman: man
quli'bua'zi: sealskin coat
se'ko: prayer
shendeek: three
si'kane'su: whale
tapooteek: boat
tehobosheen: star
tu: small blanket for a child
winum: dead
woasut: Beothuk woman or wife
wobee: white
woodum: pond or lake
yaseek: one

Bibliography

Anger, Dorothy. *Noywa'Mkisk (Where the sand Blows): Vignettes of Bay St. George Micmacs.* Port au Port East: Bay St. George Regional Indian Band Council, 1988.

Assiniwi, Bernard. *The Beothuk Saga.* Translated by Wayne Grady. McClelland and Stewart, 1996.

Beckel, Annamarie. *All Gone Widdun.* St. John's: Breakwater Books, 1999.

Collins, Gary: *Mattie Mitchell: Newfoundland's Greatest Frontiersman.* Paradise: Flanker Press, 2011.

Cormack, W. E. *A Journey Across the Island of Newfoundland.* London, New York and Toronto: Longmans, Green and Co. Ltd., 1822.

Encyclopedia of Newfoundland and Labrador, Volume I. Joseph R. Smallwood Newfoundland Book Publishers, 1967.

Howley, James P. *The Beothucks or Red Indians*. Cambridge Press. 1915.

Marshall, Ingeborg C, L., ed. *Reports and letters by George Pulling relating to the Beothuk Indians of Newfoundland*. St. Johns: Breakwater Books, 1989.

Murray, Alexander and James Howley. *Geological Survey of Newfoundland*. London: Edward Standford, 1881.

Palsson, Hermann and Magnus Magnusson. *The Vinland Sagas: The Norse Discovery of America*. Penguin Books, 1965.

Peyton, Amy Louise. *River Lords: Father and Son*. Paradise: Flanker Press, 2005.

Rowe, Frederick W. *Extinction: The Beothuks of Newfoundland*. McGraw-Hill Ryerson Limited. 1986.

Speck, Frank Goldsmith. *Beothuk and Micmac: Indian Notes and Monographs*. 1922.

Whitby, Barbara: *A Canadian Tragedy: The Last of The Beothuk*. Altitude Publishing Canada Ltd., 2005.

Whitehead, Ruth Holmes. *The Old Man Told Us: Excerpts from Mi'Kmaw History: 1500-1950*. Halifax: Nimbus, 1991.

SANTU

Mary March (Demasduit), who was captured in 1819 and died of tuberculosis ten months later. This portrait is a miniature painted by the wife of Sir Charles Hamilton, the original of which is in the National Archives, Ottawa. Courtesy of Newfoundland Archives.

Shanawdithit (Nancy), who was taken by William Cull in 1823 and died in St. John's in 1829. She has long been believed to be the last of the Beothuk, though Kop, father of Santu, outlived her. Courtesy of Tooton's Limited.

JOE TONEY

SANTU AND HER SON JOE TONEY

Gary Collins was born in Hare Bay, Bonavista North. He spent forty years in the logging and sawmilling business with his father, Theophilus, and son Clint. Gary was once Newfoundland's youngest fisheries guardian. He managed log drives down spring rivers for years, spent seven seasons driving tractor-trailers over ice roads and the Beaufort Sea of Canada's Western Arctic, and has been involved in the crab, lobster, and cod commercial fisheries. In 2016, he joined the Canadian Rangers.

Gary's writing career began when he was asked to write eulogies for deceased friends and family. Now a critically acclaimed author, he has written twelve books, including the children's illustrated book *What Colour is the Ocean?*, which he co-wrote with his granddaughter, Maggie Rose Parsons. That book won an Atlantic Book Award: The Lillian Shepherd Memorial Award for Excellence in Illustration. His book *Mattie Mitchell: Newfoundland's Greatest Frontiersman* has been adapted for film.

Gary Collins is Newfoundland and Labrador's favourite storyteller, and today he is known all over the province as "the Story Man." His favourite pastimes are reading, writing, and playing guitar at his log cabin. He lives in Hare Bay, Newfoundland, with his wife, the former Rose Gill. They have three children and three grandchildren.

ALSO BY GARY COLLINS

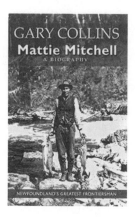

Mattie Mitchell: Newfoundland's Greatest Frontiersman
ISBN: 9781926881010

"There is a feeling that comes to one who goes unafraid into the wilderness. For the very few who experience it comes a sense of belonging; of being a fragile part of the mysterious whole; of profound peace; of wanting never to leave," says Gary Collins in describing the inspiration that overtook him when he penned the final pages in this, the biography of Mattie Mitchell, a hunter, trapper, and guide of Mi'kmaq descent whose daring feats became known worldwide.

In researching the life and times of Mattie Mitchell, critically acclaimed author Gary Collins (author of the award-winning *What Colour is the Ocean?*) gleaned much insight on his subject from the diary and other personal papers of Marie Sparkes, granddaughter to the remarkable Mi'kmaq woodsman. Now, for the first time, Mattie Mitchell's legendary deeds are revealed in full, comprehensive detail.

WWW.FLANKERPRESS.COM

ALSO BY GARY COLLINS

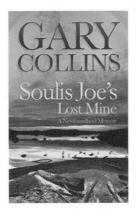

Soulis Joe's Lost Mine
ISBN: 9781897317389

Embedded in a rock in an obscure, pristine brook in the wilds of Newfoundland is a legendary quartz vein. The source of the legend is Soulis (Suley) Joe, and the precious metal trapped in the vein is silver. Along the Trans-Canada Highway in Newfoundland, just west of the turnoff to Benton, is a brook called Soulis Brook, which flows out of Soulis Pond, the second major pond named after Soulis Joe, an intrepid explorer whose name is recorded for all time on old Newfoundland maps.

In the summer of 2008, writer Gary Collins teamed up with Allan Keats, a great-grandson of Soulis Joe, and they set out to unearth the secret of Soulis Joe's lost silver mine. After many weeks and months spent combing the island of Newfoundland, Gary Collins figured it out. Come along for the trip and discover the location of Soulis Joe's Lost Mine.

WWW.FLANKERPRESS.COM

ALSO BY GARY COLLINS

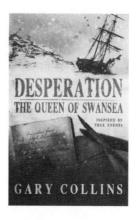

Desperation: The Queen of Swansea
ISBN: 9781771175517

Shipwreck. Starvation. Cannibalism.

For the first time, celebrated author Gary Collins brings to life the tale of the brigantine *Queen of Swansea*. Bound for Newfoundland in December 1867, the vessel made her first port of call in St. John's, only to meet her doom on the rocks of Gull Island, Cape John.

The following spring, Captain Mark Rowsell of Leading Tickles chanced upon the fallen ship's crew on his return voyage from the seal hunt. His discovery of the wreckage, and the fate of the men and women on board, marks a chilling and unforgettable event that has echoed worldwide in the history of seagoing vessels. Here, Gary Collins recreates the final voyage of the *Queen of Swansea* in a story with a gruesome turn of events that makes it unique in the annals of Atlantic shipwrecks.

WWW.FLANKERPRESS.COM

ALSO BY GARY COLLINS

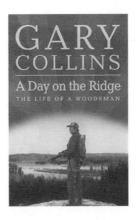

A Day on the Ridge: The Life of a Woodsman
ISBN: 9781771170406

Among the bays, inlets, and communities of the province, author Gary Collins has earned a seat at the head of the table as Newfoundland and Labrador's favourite storyteller. Now, the "Story Man" from Hare Bay is ready to tell you a little bit about himself. The tales that make up this volume are pockets of memories taken from diary entries he recorded during the forty years he spent as a woodsman. Beginning with his childhood, Gary Collins retraces his first steps as a boy growing up in Bonavista North in the 1950s, when his father taught him the skills of an outdoorsman and how to be a leader of men.

These twenty-two stories are a testimony of the hardiness of men who work amid leaf and bough, and a tribute to the call of the wild that draws these hunters, trappers, and woodcutters back to "the ridge." *A Day on the Ridge* is Gary Collins's first purely autobiographical work.

WWW.FLANKERPRESS.COM

ALSO BY GARY COLLINS

A Time That Was: Christmas in Newfoundland
ISBN: 9781771173650

A collection of true Christmas stories by Gary Collins, Newfoundland and Labrador's favourite storyteller!

Gary Collins invites us to live again the gone forever. These stories embody the soul of Christmas in outport Newfoundland, and each one carries a message that rings true every time: all roads lead to home.

Christmas, with all its lights and music and gift giving, is also a time to remember days long ago. Community togetherness and the strength of family come alive in these pages, where Gary Collins, in his inimitable style, reminds us of the poverty of possession and the wealth of sharing.

WWW.FLANKERPRESS.COM

ALSO BY GARY COLLINS

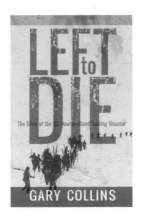

Left to Die
ISBN: 9781771173285

Cecil Mouland, one of the last living survivors of the SS *Newfoundland* sealing disaster, told his story to Gary Collins in the fall of 1971 while travelling to St. John's, where the old ice hunter would live out his final days. This book grew from that encounter and stands alone as the defining tale of the men who were left to die on the ice.

The historic convergence of ice, seals, and men in late March 1914 marked the end of Newfoundland's innocence. Men both young and old left their homes from all over the province that year to pursue the annual seal hunt. Among the vessels that took them to the ice was the *Newfoundland*, a wooden-walled steamship captained by the famous Captain Westbury Kean. With no wireless aboard the ship, the stage was set for seventy-eight of the men who went over the side and their fates sealed.

WWW.FLANKERPRESS.COM

INSPIRED BY TRUE EVENTS

Long after Demasduit's skull has been stolen from her grave, and years after Shanawdithit has died, one Beothuk and his family survive.

Bursting out of the pages of Newfoundland history appears Kop, the last true Beothuk.

When all the other members of his tribe are exterminated by the Europeans, Kop seeks revenge against the Unwanted Ones.

Hidden among the Bear Clan of the Mi'kmaq, the Beothuk strikes back.

Follow Kop on his trail of defiance against the European marauders upon his Island. See what becomes of a man who has nothing to lose or live for.

Stay with him on a hundred trails and sit with him across the smoke of a hundred campfires. You will not only weep for the last Beothuk—you will cheer him on as he pushes back against the Unwanted Ones.

ISBN 978-177117-632-3

9 781771 176323

$19.95

FLANKER PRESS
www.flankerpress.com
Also available as an ebook

Cover design:

graham blair
designs.com

ANCIENT FOREST FRIENDLY™ This book is printed on Ancient Forest Friendly paper